FLORA KIDD

wife by contract

Harlequin Books

TORONTO • LONDON • LOS ANGELES • AMSTERDAM
SYDNEY • HAMBURG • PARIS • STOCKHOLM • ATHENS • TOKYO

Harlequin Presents edition published December 1980
ISBN 0-373-10400-6

Original hardcover edition published in 1980
by Mills & Boon Limited

CHAPTER ONE

An antique crystal chandelier hung from the middle of a high plaster ceiling which had been carved long ago with a pattern of roses and cupids. The same pattern had been carved on the warm wooden panelling of the room. It was a beautiful room, once the ballroom of an elegant Regency house in the West End of London, but now there was roulette in it instead of the sound of violins and graceful measured dancing.

There were four tables. The biggest crowd was around the table nearest the centre of the room, almost directly under the chandelier, and it was towards that table that a dark-haired, wide-shouldered man who was dressed in formal black and white dinner clothes walked slowly yet purposefully, his hands thrust in the pockets of his well-tailored trousers.

As he approached the table another man, his fair face flushed and his grey eyes sparkling with anger, pushed his way out of the crowd.

"What's happening?" asked the dark man.

"She's losing and she won't give up," replied the younger man. "I can't get her to leave the table, so I've told her I'm going home. That should make her stop."

He marched off, and the dark man went on to stand behind the group of men and women who were watching, his gaze fixing on the young woman who was sitting on the other side of the wheel.

She had a lot of silvery blond hair. It was drawn back from her high rounded forehead and held in the middle of her head by a wide bandeau of black velvet. Behind the bandeau it hung in a mass of carefully disordered ringlets to her shoulders, which were bare except for the narrow strips of black silk holding up the bodice of her dress.

Light glittered in her white-gold hair and gleamed on the smooth ivory-tinted skin of her shoulders, casting a deep shadow in the cleft which divided her breasts. Her face was very pale and the pink tip of her tongue pushed at the lower lip of her softly curved lips. Long mascaraed eyelashes quivered about her dark blue eyes as she stared at the spinning roulette wheel.

It was slowing down and Teri Hayton's lips parted slowly as she watched the little ivory ball drift down the curve of the wheel and bounce on the ridges above the numbers. Then it stopped with a click. The wheel slowed even more, carrying the ball around with it. When the wheel stopped revolving completely the croupier announced the winning number.

There was a shriek of triumphant laughter from a woman sitting on Teri's left. She had won for the first time that evening. The croupiers reached out to collect up the chips. Teri watched her last bet go with the rest. Now she was in even more of a mess than she had been when she had first come to this club earlier in the week, determined to win enough money to pay off the enormous debt which her father had left when he had died recently. Now she had not only lost her savings but she was also in debt to the club, which had covered her bets this evening.

Looking around, she caught the croupier's eye and arched her eyebrows at him enquiringly as he asked people to place their bets again. He shook his head slowly from side to side. That meant the house wouldn't cover any more of her bets. Teri's glance moved on around the people who were watching. Jim had gone as he had threatened he would. She was alone and would have to find her way back to Richmond as best she could.

Standing up, she excused herself and turned away from the table. Tall, her slender figure seeming slimmer in the clinging black gown, she made her way out of the room and went down the curving staircase to the entrance hall, moving slowly and gracefully, her bright head held high, a faint smile tilting her lips, refusing to show to the world that she was desperate.

At the cloakroom in the hallway she presented a ticket and the woman in charge brought her a long black velvet evening cloak which was lined with oyster-coloured satin. Teri was just about to lift the cloak from the counter and swing it about her shoulders when an arm clothed in smooth black barathea stretched in front of her.

"Allow me," said a quiet masculine voice.

She turned quickly, her finely plucked eyebrows arching haughtily. The man was only slightly taller than herself. He had very wide shoulders and a broad chest. Above the collar of his white evening shirt his square-chinned face was olive-skinned and on either side of his bold downward-curving nose his eyes were very dark, almost black, set beneath thick, strangely peaked eyebrows. Lustrous black hair coiled on his broad sloping forehead and grew down the sides of his lean cheeks.

"Thank you," she said coolly, and turning her back to him let him place the cloak over her shoulders. He seemed familiar, but she couldn't think for the moment where they had met. "Do I know you?" she asked, turning back to him as she fastened the long velvet ties of her cloak in a bow beneath her chin.

"You know of me, I expect, but we haven't been introduced," he replied politely, and although his English was perfect there was a crispness to the words which made her suspect he hadn't learned it in England. "I've been watching you play this evening... and other evenings," he added.

So that was where she had seen him, standing among the others who had crowded around the table. He had been like a black moth hovering among brilliantly winged butterflies, somewhat sinister and— Teri gave him a fleeting glance—and satanic. She felt a tingle of apprehension go through her and decided she must get away from him, so giving him her coolest and most dismissing look she said,

"Thank you again. Goodnight."

She turned on her heel and made for the panelled front door, smiling graciously at the doorman when he opened it for her. She stepped out in the lamplit night and the door closed behind her. For a moment she lingered, feeling the raw damp wind whip through the velvet cloak, chilling her bare skin, and wishing she had left when Jim had, wishing she could afford a taxi to take her to Richmond.

"I'd be glad to drive you anywhere you wish to go."

The dark man was there right beside her, yet Teri was sure he hadn't been with her when she had stepped through the door. She took fright suddenly and hurried down the steps, not looking where she was going, her glance sweeping the street in search of the taxi. On the bottom step the heel of her black patent evening sandal turned under her and she lost balance. The man was beside her immediately, a hand on her arm, helping her to her feet.

"There's an English saying, isn't there, that pride always comes before a fall," he mocked. "And you are proud, so proud you won't admit to yourself that you're in one hell of a mess."

"How do you know I am?" she demanded, turning on him and wrenching her arm free from his grasp. Deeply shadowed in the street lighting, his face seemed even more satanic. "Who are you? The devil?" she exclaimed.

His laughter was softly scoffing and she felt the hairs rise on her neck.

"Perhaps I am your particular devil right now," he drawled. "The name is Damien Nikerios. I believe it must be familiar to you. I'm here in London to meet you. In fact I've been trying to meet you for two weeks, but you've proved to be very elusive. There are matters to be discussed and arranged...."

"There is nothing to be discussed or arranged between us, Mr. Nikerios," she retorted. "I intend to pay back the money you lent my father, don't worry. The devil will get his due. Goodnight."

Once again she turned her back on him and began to march along the street, but she didn't get very far alone. Within a few seconds he was walking along beside her, moving easily with long strides, hands in the pocket of his trousers.

"Do you intend to walk all the way to where you live?" he asked pleasantly.

"No. I shall take the Underground to Waterloo Station and from there I shall take a train to Richmond," she said coolly.

"Is that safe for you, at this time of night, dressed as you are?" he said.

"What do you mean, dressed as I am?" She swung towards him, pulling her cloak closely and shivering slightly. It was really very cold, cold enough for snow, even though it was late March and almost spring time.

"That dress you are wearing is very revealing, provocative, one might say," he drawled suggestively. "And a woman like you, alone at night, could be on the receiving end of some unpleasant attentions from some unpleasant people."

"Look, Mr. Nikerios," she replied, speaking to him with the sort of weary patience the native of a country often uses to a foreign visitor, "this is my town and I've been travelling by Underground for many years late at night, and nothing unpleasant has ever happened to me yet."

"There's always a first time. I have a car parked on a street near here and as I said before, I'll be glad to drive you. We could talk on the way." He noticed her shiver again. "You'd be much warmer and safer...."

"With Damien Nikerios?" she interrupted acidly. "I doubt it. Your reputation with women is well known."

"You're very like him," he said quietly, ignoring her jibe.

"Like whom?"

"Alex... your father. Proud, reckless, independent. He was a great guy," he went on softly. "You and he must have been good friends. I bet you miss him."

"Oh, I do, I do!" It was an involuntary response to the first kind comment anyone outside her family had made about her father since he had died. The next second she was all pride again, her head up. "We were good friends. That's why I can't understand why he didn't tell me about his arrangement with you."

"I could explain, but not here. It's too cold. If you won't let me drive you will you come and have some supper? There's a small restaurant near here. We could have a drink and something to eat and then you can go back to Richmond."

"And if I refuse? What will you do?" Teri challenged.

"I'll walk with you to the Underground station, travel with you to Waterloo and then to Richmond. Now that I've caught up with you I'm not letting you out of my sight until we have come to some sensible arrangement."

"You really like to have your own way, don't you?" she taunted, but the taunt lost much of its sharpness because her teeth chattered suddenly with cold.

"No more than you do," he replied equably.

For a few moments she struggled with her pride. After all, she had managed to avoid meeting this man for two weeks now and had sworn she wouldn't have anything to do with him. But she was hungry and very cold and there was something about him, a warm sympathy reaching out to her in spite of his satanic appearance, which attracted her.

"All right." She gave in abruptly. "But I must catch the last train."

"You will," he said. "This way."

It wasn't far to the restaurant and to step in through its doorway was to be transported from the dismal darkness of the March night into the bright sunshine of Greece. Under glowing golden lighting rough white walls sparkled and warm floor tiles glowed. Multi-coloured ikons and tapestries hung on the walls and from speakers, concealed somewhere, came the rhythmic beat of *bouzouki* music. A young waiter dressed in black pants and black shirt with a cheeky red scarf tied round his neck greeted Damien Nikerios as if he were an old friend, smiled at Teri as if she were the only woman in the world, and led them through an archway into another more secluded dining area.

Taking a seat, Teri slid the cloak from her shoulders so that it was draped over the back of her chair and looked around her with interest while Damien Nikerios studied the menu.

"Are there places like this where you come from?" she asked.

"Pardon me?" He looked up from the menu, obviously having heard her speak but not having taken in the sense of what she had said.

"This place," she said. "It's supposed to be like a *taverna* in Greece, isn't it?"

He looked round the room, then looked back at her. Amusement gleamed in his eyes and pulled at his mouth.

"It's a fairly good imitation of a Greek *taverna*, yes," he replied. "Probably it's cleaner and less smelly. Have you never been to Greece?"

"No, I haven't."

"Would you like to go there?"

"Doesn't everyone? To see the Acropolis in Athens, the Sanctuary at Delphi and other ancient remains? You are Greek, aren't you?"

"Mostly Greek. Three quarters, I would guess. The other quarter is solid Anglo-Saxon. My father is, of course, wholly Greek, but my mother is of mixed Greek and American descent and she's told me often enough that I'm very like her father. He was a New Englander and claimed that one of his forebears signed the Declaration of Independence."

"But you're not like him in looks, surely," Teri remarked.

"No. In temperament. Stubborn as a mule, she calls me." His crooked smile was self-mocking. "What would you like to eat?"

"Would it be possible for me to have an omelette?"

"I'll ask."

The young waiter came back with a bottle of clear liquor and two glasses. Damien Nikerios spoke to him in Greek and after placing a dish of titbits on the table, cheese, olives, slices of fish and meat, he answered in the same language as he poured liquor into the glasses.

"He says the chef will be delighted to make an omelette for such a lovely lady as you," said Damien Nikerios, amusement rippling the usually smooth flow of his deep voice. "Any particular filling?"

"Mushrooms, please, if there are any," replied Teri, and smiled at the waiter.

"Madam, for you I will go and pick them myself," he said flamboyantly, bowing to her with his hand over his heart, flashing his eyes and his perfect white teeth at her.

"You've obviously made a conquest there," murmured Damien Nikerios when the waiter had gone. He picked up his glass and raised it. "To our better acquaintance," he drawled.

"What is it?" she asked, eyeing the glass of liquor suspiciously.

"*Ouzo*. It tastes of aniseed."

"Won't it go to my head?"

"Try it and see," he replied, gazing at her, the blackness of his lashes making his eyes seem even darker and conveniently hiding any expression in them.

She sipped it a little. He was right, the drink did taste of aniseed and seemed innocuous enough. She helped herself to some of the titbits and drank a little more.

"Were you really hoping to win enough money at roulette this week to pay off the debt your father owed to me?" he asked.

"Yes. It was a long shot, a gamble I had to take," she replied, and drank some more *ouzo*. She was beginning to feel warm at last and less afraid of the man who was sitting opposite to her. He wasn't quite so devilish-looking as he had first appeared to her and she realised now that her own desperate feelings when she had been leaving the gambling club had caused her to distort his looks.

"Why?" he asked bluntly.

"Well, I had to try and do something," she blurted. "You see, I can't possibly let you take everything from us, the house where my mother lives, the shares which my father owned in Hayton's which she and I and my brother Dick should have inherited and which my father offered to you as security when he borrowed from you. Dad's death was a great shock to us...."

"I'm sure it was," he murmured, lifting the bottle of *ouzo* and refilling his own glass and hers. "And I'm truly sorry it happened the way it did. A car accident, wasn't it?"

'Yes."

"I was shocked too, when I heard of it."

"Then why didn't you come to his funeral if you thought so highly of him?" she retorted.

"Because I didn't get news of his death until after the funeral was over, when his lawyer wrote to me reminding me of the terms on which Alex had borrowed the money from me," he replied calmly. "I came as soon as I could and went to see the lawyers." He gave her a level underbrowed glance. "They tried to contact your mother, but were told she had gone away and did not wish to see me. They were also told you did not wish to see me. That was when I asked for the address of your home and drove out to Richmond. No one was at home. There has been no one home for the past two weeks." His mouth curved sardonically.

"Mother was ill, shocked not only by Dad's death but also by the knowledge that unless the debt was paid off she would be turned out of her home and thateverything would be yours," Teri rushed in breathlessly and defensively. "She went awayto Manchester, to stay with her sister."

"At your suggestion, I suppose," he drawled dryly. "What about your brother?"

"Dick? Oh, he went back to school. He's only seventeen and has to finish his education so he can go into the business. He's a boarder at Brookhill School. That's in Dorset, if you really must know."

"And where have you been hiding these past two weeks?" he demanded sharply.

The autocratic tone of voice made her bristle. Taking her time, she picked up her glass and drank the rest of the *ouzo*, staring at him defiantly as she did so. Setting down the empty glass, she picked up her evening bag.

"I've been staying with a friend," she replied coolly.

"The young man who was at the gambling club with you?" he asked. "He seemed pretty angry with you tonight, so angry he walked out on you. Do you live with him?"

"With Jim? Good heavens, no!" She laughed a little as she took a packet of cigarettes out of her bag. "I've been staying with his sister, Shirley Russel. She and I are close friends. We went to school together. I asked Jim to go with me to the club because I know the management there don't like to let women in who are unescorted."

"How much did you lose?"

"That's none of your business," she retorted, selecting a cigarette. She closed the packet, dropped it into her handbag and began to search for her lighter.

"All your savings, which would amount to a few hundred pounds, I would guess, plus the thousand you borrowed from the management."

"How do you know about that?" she demanded, flushing angrily.

"Never mind how I know. I do. So now *you're* in debt." His tone was critical. "Wouldn't it have been wiser to hang on to your savings and wait until you had heard what I intend to do before throwing your money away on the wheel of fortune?"

"I suppose it would, but you see I'm not very wise," she replied airily. The *ouzo* had gone to her head. She felt giddy and careless. "I'm like Alex," she went on. "Proud, reckless and far too independent to be beholden to someone like you."

"Proud, reckless and beautiful," he murmured. "A dangerous mixture." His dark eyes seemed suddenly soft and sensuous as their gaze lingered on her throat before drifting down to the cleft between her breasts revealed by the low cut of her bodice, and she felt nerves in the soft mounds of flesh quiver and tauten as if he had touched her possessively. Alarmed by this reaction to his glance, she put the cigarette in her mouth, but before she could even flick her lighter into flame he reached a long arm across the table and snapped the cigarette from between her lips.

"Why did you do that?" she demanded angrily as he broke the cigarette in half between strong dark fingers.

"You didn't ask me if you could smoke," he said coldly, giving her a look of pure distaste as he broke the two halves of the cigarette again and dropped them into the ashtray. "I prefer not to have my food ruined by the smoke of someone else's tobacco."

"In that case you can eat by yourself!" she flared, and pushed to her feet.

"Sit down," he ordered, menace gleaming in the darkness of his eyes, his lips hardly moving as he spoke.

"No, I won't!"

"If you dare to take one step away from the table I'll get hold of you and drag you back. And don't think that's an idle threat. I've created more scenes in public places than I care to remember. Now sit down and behave yourself."

No one had spoken to Teri like that in her life. Her father's darling, her mother's pet, her young brother's adored elder sister, she had never been crossed by anyone in her family. Always she had had her own way, and so for a moment she wavered, glaring down at him. He returned her glare coolly, his face rockhard, his mouth set in a grim line, both of his hands spread on the table, ready to push him to his feet.

Then suddenly the young waiter was there, tray held high at his shoulder.

"You are getting impatient, madam," he said jokingly in his broken English. "It took me a long time to pick the mushrooms. But here we are at last—an omelette fit for a goddess to eat. Mmm, delicious!''

With a flourish he set a plate in her place and, her hunger aggravated by the sight and smell of the fluffy golden omelette, Teri sank down on her chair again. She found she was shaking all over and had a most unusual desire to burst into tears because for once in her life she had been forced to give in to a man's threat.

The waiter placed a plate with something which looked like a wedge of pie on it in front of Damien Nikerios and then proceeded to open a bottle of white wine he had brought. He poured the wine and left them. Rather sullenly Teri picked up her knife and fork and began to eat. After a while she said without looking up,

"As I'd guessed, you're a bully. I suppose that being mostly Greek you regard women as inferior persons who must be kept in their place.''

"It's becoming very apparent to me that Alex never spanked you when you were young," he retorted smoothly.

"Of course he didn't," she replied indignantly. "He was much too gentle and tolerant to use corporal punishment.''

"Mmm. He was easy-going, and I suppose that is why he got into financial difficulties," he said musingly. "How is the omelette?''

"Very good...thank you," she said stiltedly, giving him a surreptitious look. She was finding his sardonic remarks disconcerting. "What's that you're eating?'' she asked.

"*Tyropita*. It's a sort of cheese pie. Have you tried the wine yet?''

She hadn't, so she lifted her glass and sipped. The wine was light and sparkling.

"It is a wine of which I'm told the British are very fond," Damien Nikerios said. "It's called *Theotokis* and is made on the island of Corfu. Do you like it?"

"Yes." She drank some more. "Why did you lend Alex so much money? Did you hope to take over Hayton's one day?"

"I lent it to him to help dig him out of the mess he had got into and to save the business from going under."

"When?"

"Six years ago. We were both in New York at the time. He was trying to get an American company interested in financing Hayton's. He wasn't having much success, so I offered to back him." He laid his knife and fork together on his empty plate, then sipped some wine. "Is it true he never told you about it?"

"Yes, it is."

His dark glance drifted over her interestedly.

"I suppose six years ago he felt you were too young to know." His eyes crinkled at the corners as a faint smile curled his mouth. "When I first met Alex you were about nine years old, I guess. I was twenty-one. I remember he was very proud of you and showed your photograph to everyone. Even at that age you were beautiful, your skin like alabaster and your hair like flax."

His direct openly admiring gaze was having the most devastating effect on her. All her bones seemed to be melting and she had the most absurd desire to lean towards him, to reach out a hand to him and feel his hand close around it. She wanted to kiss him and have him kiss her....

Her breath rasped in her throat and she seized her glass. She gulped down the wine quickly and felt it seep through her.

"Where did you meet him—the first time, I mean?" she croaked.

He leaned forward, picked up the wine bottle and refilled both glasses before he answered.

"At the house of an archaeologist who had done some interesting excavations of a temple on Skios, the island my father owns and where he now lives. The archaeologist had written a book about his finds and Alex had come to see him to talk about publishing it." He lifted his glass and drank some wine. "While he was there, Alex gave me some good advice which I took... eventually. I have never forgotten the way he talked to me. He saved me from making a fool of myself."

"Over what?" Teri was surprised. So far he had not struck her as being the sort of person who would ever make a fool of himself.

"Over a woman." His expression was cynical as he studied the wine in his glass. Then he lifted his wide shoulders in a dismissing shrug. "But that's past history and best forgotten. All that matters is Alex did me a good turn once and so when he needed help I was only too glad to lend him money."

"At a price, of course," she sniped. "No one would ever expect the son of Stephanos Nikerios to lend money without demanding some sort of security first." Recklessly she ignored the dangerous narrowing of his eyes and rushed on. "Poor Daddy," she said feelingly, "he must have been really desperate to agree to your terms, you... you vulture!"

"Prejudiced bitch, aren't you?" The softly spoken insult rocked her in her chair.

"I'm not!" she retorted hotly.

"Sure you are. You've made up your mind about me and nothing I say is going to change it, so I might as well save my breath." He finished the wine in his glass and then pushing aside his plate leaned forward with his folded arms on the table. "Now let's get down to business and consider the situation as it exists. Of the amount of money I lent to Alex two hundred thousand pounds is still owing to me. Right?"

She nodded and fiddled with the stem of her wine glass.

"So, according to the terms of the agreement which he and I signed—at his insistence, I should add—in the event of his death or his being unable to pay back the loan, I take over not only the house where your mother lives but also the virtual control of the publishing company, thus disinheriting your mother, you and your brother. Right again?"

"Not if I can help it," she said between set teeth, gripping the stem of the glass. She longed to throw the contents into his face. "Not if there's some way to avoid that happening."

"You mean that?" he asked.

"I do, most sincerely. I'd do anything to stop you from taking everything away from my mother and my brother."

The hard line of his mouth relaxed and the cold glitter went out of his eyes as his glance once again drifted over her admiringly, almost seductively.

"There is a way," he murmured, and she found herself thinking about his mouth. It puzzled her. Its shape changed according to what he was thinking or feeling. Right now its curves were frankly sensual. But there was sweetness there too, and humour, yet only a few moments ago his lips had been tight with anger. Teri wondered what it would be like to feel them moving against hers... God, what was she doing? The wine must be going to her head now, loosening her control over her senses. She blinked and sat up stiffly.

"What way?" she said.

"You and I could make a new arrangement."

"What sort of an arrangement?" Oh, now she was very much on guard, having read of his affairs with women. The blood pounded in her ears. If he asked her to be his mistress she would throw the wine at him, she vowed, the glass too, and then she would walk out.

"If you agree to marry me I won't demand that the remaining outstanding two hundred thousand be paid to me, nor shall I turn your mother out of her house and take over Alex's share in Hayton's which by right of inheritance should be divided between your mother and your brother," he said.

Teri stared at him with her mouth slightly open, the intention to throw the wine at him completely forgotten in complete surprise.

"You can't be serious!" she croaked.

"I am serious. I'm sober too, in case you have any doubts on that score," he added with that attractive lift to one corner of his mouth as her glance went uncertainly to his empty glass. "This isn't just a spur-of-the-moment proposal, Teri. It's a way for you to keep the publishing business in the Hayton family. My money put Hayton's back on its feet six years ago. I still have a certain amount invested in the business which I'm willing to leave inprovided I receive some dividend. As my wife you would be that."

for his due. She drank more wine and looked at him again, feeling at once the force of his attraction. If she married him she would have everything any woman could ever want—money, luxury, even a certain sort of power. It was tempting, very tempting. Could she do it?

"Have you ever been married before?" she asked cautiously.

"No. Have you?"

"No...I was going to be, two years ago, but...he was killed." She seemed to be having some difficulty in forming her words. "Another car accident," she muttered. "I hate cars. Two people I loved most in the world killed by cars...." She broke off, her hand going to her mouth. She was becoming maudlin and the walls seemed to be moving, closing in on her. Everything seemed to be tilting about her, first one way then the other. The candlelight was dancing up and up in high blue-centred yellow flames and above them she could see a dark devilish face with glinting black eyes watching her. Her stomach was heaving and her head was expanding and contracting. Rising to her feet, she muttered some excuse about having to go to the ladies' room.

Through the archway she went, weaving between the tables on her way to the door of the restaurant. She could hear someone speaking to her, calling her name, but she went on, determined to get away, thinking that fresh air would clear her head.

Out through the door she went. The cold damp air stung her bare shoulders and arms and instead of clearing her head made it spin. Flakes of something soft were falling in a white haze, covering the pavement, flicking her skin like feathers. Snow. It was snowing and she had come out without her cloak. She had best go back for it. She turned, bumped into someone, felt something hit her hard on the head and then was whirling downwards, sucked in by the vortex of oblivion.

CHAPTER TWO

TERI was wakened by the sound of a door closing. Opening her eyes, she saw a long window divided by strips of wood into square panes of glass. Through the panes she could see the sun. It was a round crimson ball hanging in a sky streaked with pink fluffy clouds behind the dark brown tracery of a tree's leafless branches.

Her eyes closed again and she turned over, stretching lazily, snuggling her head into a soft down pillow. She felt drowsily content, relaxed in a way she had never felt before. She felt she was floating on feathery clouds...feathers? A frown pleated her high forehead. When had she felt feathers flicking against her face and her shoulders? Last night. It had been snowing when she had stepped out of the Greek restaurant where she had had supper with the devil.

In one movement she turned and sat up to gaze wildly at the window again. The window of the house where she normally lived didn't face east. Nor did it face south or west. It faced north, so she could never see the sun from it at any time of the day. The bedroom she had been sleeping in at Shirley's didn't have a window like the one she could see through now, nor was there a tree outside it. She was in a room she had never seen before, a luxuriously furnished room with two long sash windows draped in green velvet, and she was lying in a king-sized bed beneath a silk-covered duvet.

Where was she? And how had she got there? Lying back against the pillows, she watched the sun slowly change colour, becoming less crimson and more orange and the feathery clouds change from pink to a pale greyish blue. There was a faint soreness at the back of her head and although she felt rested and thoroughly relaxed there was a dryness in her mouth and a dull throb behind her eyes.

Slowly, as if afraid of what she might find beneath it, she lifted the duvet. She was wearing a dark blue pyjama jacket; a man's pyjama jacket. It was made of some silky material and it covered her to her knees. She dropped the duvet back into place and looked again around the room. The furniture was handsome, custom-made, she guessed. There was a wide dressing table with a triple mirror, a chest of drawers and a huge wardrobe with a long mirror in its door. The room was very tidy. No clothes were draped over the chairs. Her glance came back to the bed and fixed on two pieces of black silk, then slid away from them to the pillow next to the one she was lying on. Her mouth seemed to become even dryer when she saw the dent in it which could have only been caused by someone's head resting there.

Panic flickered through her sharply, destroying the feeling of delicious lassitude in her limbs. She sat up again and reached for the pieces of black silk. As she had suspected, they were the top and pants of a pair of men's pyjamas. Inside the collar of the jacket there was a label bearing the name of the maker. Underneath it was a name tag. D. Nikerios.

Teri stared at the name. So she hadn't dreamt it. She had slept with Damien Nikerios last night. *And not only slept.* A knock on the door made her jump guiltily. Pushing the black pyjamas under the duvet, she slid down under it and waited. The knock came again. She didn't answer but watched the door open slowly. A thin middle-aged woman with iron-grey hair who was wearing a neat wine-red dress entered. She was carrying a tray on which there was a silver tea service and a china cup and saucer. She set the tray down on the bedside table and looked over at Teri, who pretended to be waking up.

"Good morning, miss," the woman spoke with a pronounced Scottish accent. "I hope you're feeling better now. Mr. Nikerios said I was to bring you some tea and to ask if you want any breakfast. He tells me you had a wee stomach upset last night. Perhaps a poached egg?"

"No. No, thank you. At least not yet. I'll just have the tea," said Teri, not moving but watching the woman warily. "Is he...I mean, where is Mr. Nikerios?" she whispered.

"Downstairs, in Sir Arthur's study. He's making some phone calls." The woman frowned slightly as she gazed at Teri's pale face. "Are you sure now you wouldn't like some thin Hovis bread toasted with butter? You're looking awful peaked and wan, so you are, and it could be something plain and simple would settle your stomach for you."

"All right, that sounds very nice," Teri whispered, and the woman nodded and smiled approvingly at her before leaving the room.

Once the door had closed Teri sat up again and edged over to the bedside table, and reached for the tea-pot. When she had poured some she picked up the cup and sipped some of the hot liquid. It eased the dryness in her mouth and throat, so she poured more and holding the cup in her hand leaned back against the headboard of the bed.

It was all coming back to her now. When she had left the restaurant she had collapsed in the street and when she had come round she had been in a car, sitting in the front next to Damien Nikerios, who had been driving. She had wanted to ask him where he had been taking her, but her head had ached so much she had been unable to make the effort to speak. Snowflakes had whirled towards the windshield in a monotonous formation and the wipers had clicked rhythmically in time to the throbbing in her head.

The car had stopped at last and Damien had got out. He had opened the door beside her, helped her out of the car and with his arm about her to support her, had guided her up some steps and through a doorway into the wide hallway of a house. But when he had urged her towards some stairs she had refused to go, so he had swung her up into his arms and had carried her.

It had been good to be carried by him because his arms had been strong. She had laid her head against his shoulder and had put her arms about his neck because when she had done that she felt better. He had carried her into this room and had set her on her feet, but she had swayed and had clung to him.

"I feel awfully sick," she had muttered, and the next thing she remembered, with a shudder, she had been in a bathroom feeling very, very ill.

After vomiting she had felt so wretched she hadn't put up any resistance when Damien Nikerios had helped her to take off her evening gown and he sisted her to put on one of his pyja been so weak she hadn't care her up again, had carried her laid her down on it and h vet. She had felt so mis had moved away she had cried to him to stay with her and had been too weary to object when he had climbed into bed beside her. After that she had fallen asleep.

Some time in the night she had dreamed of David whom she had loved so much and whom she had been going to marry. It was a dream which she had had several times since he had been killed. She had dreamt he had been in bed beside her, but as soon as she had turned to him and put her arms about him he had faded into nothing and she had awakened cold and unhappy to find her arms empty.

Last night had been different. Last night when she had spoken his name a voice had answered her, a warm deep voice which had held an undercurrent of laughter.

"The name is Damien, not David," it had said.

Still half dreaming, Teri hadn't believed it, and turning towards the sound of the voice she had stretched out an arm. Her hand had touched the softness of silk stretched across a warm pulsing body. Sliding down over the hard rib-cage, her fingers had curved happily about the lean tensile waist and had explored even further over the flatness of a stomach until she had heard someone catch their breath and had felt fingers curl around her wrist and lift her hand away.

"If you're going to do things like that I'll have to leave you," the voice had whispered.

"No, no. Oh, please don't leave me," she had cried out, and putting her arms out had wound them 'und his neck. "Please stay. Hold me and keep me ᵔn't go away!"

ᵉcted him to fade away then as he al- instead there was movement and she had been gathered by strong arms against the warm chest.

"Like that?" he had whispered, and his breath had been hot against her temple.

"Yes, like that," she had replied, and had come fully awake and had recognised him.

"What are you doing here?" she had asked, but she hadn't tried to move away. She had been too warm and comfortable.

"You asked me to stay with you," he had murmured.

"Did you mean it when you said if I marry you you won't take everything away from us?" she had asked.

"I meant it."

"I thought you were going to ask me to be your mistress," she had said with a little laugh, and had snuggled her head into his shoulder.

"I know you did."

"Oh. You seem to know everything," she had replied, lifting her head and trying to see him, but it had been impossible to see more than a dark shape. "Why do you want to marry me?"

"Because I like the way you look," he had answered, and she had felt his fingers trail delicately down her throat and rest in the V-opening of the pyjama jacket as if in readiness to undo the top button.

"That isn't a good reason for marriage," she had argued drowsily. The warmth of his body seemed to melt hers so that it had moulded itself to his shape. She had lifted a hand and had groped for his face, had found it, had slid her fingers gently over the high boss of a cheekbone down to his mouth. Delicately her forefinger had traced the enigmatic shape of his lips. "I wish you would kiss me," she had whispered. "I've been longing all evening for you to kiss me."

"You're sure you can take the consequences if I do?" His voice had throbbed strangely and he had slipped undone the top button of the pyjama jacket. Against the coolness of her skin his fingers had been hot as they had searched for tender nerve endings and had found them.

"Are you seducing me?" she had breathed shakily as a tingle of excruciating yet pleasurable pain had danced along her nerves.

"No more than you are seducing me," he had replied tantalisingly. "Will you marry me?"

"Only if you'll kiss me, now," she had groaned. "Please, oh, please do it now!"

His lips had been hot against hers yet gentle too, hardening with passion only when she had responded, and after that there had been no turning back as both of them had given in to the strong tide of sensuousness which had swept through them, hurling them onwards towards the culmination of ecstasy and which had not ebbed until they had both lain lax in drowsy contentment in each other's arms.

"And so, now I have kissed you, will you marry me?" he had murmured, and the undercurrent of laughter had been back in his voice.

"Oh, yes, yes, I will," she had whispered, and had let the tears of release fall from her eyes to wet her cheeks and his.

Teri's hands shook and drops of tea splashed down on the duvet. She tipped the cup towards her mouth and drank. Then setting it down on the saucer she rolled off the bed and walked over to one of the windows. It overlooked a garden surrounded by a wall built of mellow yellowish-red London bricks which was covered this morning with a thin gauze of snow already melting under the rays of the sun. The tree she had seen from the bed, streaking the sun with its dark bare branches was a tall elm, one of the few which had escaped disease, and it was standing, frosted with snow, in the park beyond the garden wall; a park she recognised only too well as a section of the extensive Hyde Park.

Whose house was this? Did it belong to Damien Nikerios? Wealthy as he was, he could afford to have houses scattered throughout the world. In fact she knew that his father had houses in Monte Carlo, in Florida and California. Slowly she went back to the bed and sitting on the edge of it poured herself some more tea. She was sipping from the delicate china cup when there was a knock at the door. It opened and the woman with the grey hair and wine-red dress came in, carrying a plate of toast and a gown over her other arm.

"Och, ye can't be feeling so bad after all," she said with a smile. "I've brought one of milady's dressing gowns for you to wear." She placed the bright red velour dressing gown on the bed and set the plate of toast on the tray. "It should fit you fine. Mr. Nikerios tells me there's been some sort of delay about your luggage and so you've nothing to wear but what you came in last night." She frowned anxiously. "I'm afraid your evening dress will have to go to the cleaners," she added. "Now is there anything else I can be getting for ye?"

"No...that is...could you ask Mr. Nikerios to come up here?"

"Now I can't be doing that right away because he's gone out to the City. He said I was to tell you he would be back about eleven-thirty and then he would take you to lunch...that is if your clothes have arrived by then."

"Oh." Teri glanced at the window. "Could you tell me the address of this house? I realise it's near the park, but I'm not sure of the number or the street and I'd like to ask a friend of mine to come and visit me while I'm staying here."

"It's Wemsley House, on Blakeney Street, Sir Arthur Wemsley's house. Mr. Nikerios's mother is married to Sir Arthur. But I'm sure you know that already."

"I . . . er . . . yes." Teri put her hands up to her suddenly hot cheeks. "Mrs. . . . I'm afraid I don't know your name."

"Esther MacCracken. I'm housekeeper here and my husband is the butler," said the woman briskly, whisking towards the door. "I must go and get on with my work now. If you want to phone your friend you can dial directly from this phone here." Mrs. MacCracken indicated the telephone which was on the bedside table. "And if you want to contact me you have only to push this button here." She pointed to a bellpush on the wall behind the bed. "Will you be all right for a while?" she added, giving Teri a bright twinkling glance.

"Yes, thank you."

The woman smiled and nodded again, her eyes still twinkling.

"I can hardly wait to see her ladyship's face when she hears the news," she said.

"What news?"

"About you and Mr. Nikerios. She'll be so surprised that he's going to get married at last and very pleased that it's to a nice-looking young woman like yourself."

She went out. Teri stared blankly at the glossy white-painted panels of the door, then picking up the butter-soaked toast she swung her legs up on the bed again and rested against the pillows while she munched. As she recalled what had happened in the night again her mouth twisted wryly. Damien Nikerios had been very clever, pressing her to marry him again just after he had seduced her, while she had still been hazy with the aftermath of passion and half in love with him. Clever too to tell the housekeeper that they were going to be married.

Unless she had dreamed everything that had happened. Perhaps she was dreaming now? There was one way to find out. She would phone Shirley.

It was some time before her friend answered the phone.

"Hello," said a slightly breathless voice.

"Shirl? It's me, Teri."

"At last!" Shirley raised her voice to shout above some noise in the background. "Where are you?"

"In London, at Wemsley House. Ever heard of it? It's in Blakeney Street."

'What on earth are you doing there? Mr. Cogswell at Hayton's phoned a few minutes ago to ask why you're not at the office today, and last night your mother phoned. She wanted to know if you'd heard from Mr. Nikerios yet...whoever he is." Shirley's voice grew fainter as she turned away from the mouthpiece and said something to someone who was in the room with her.

"Listen, Shirley," Teri said forcibly. "Can you come here with some of my day clothes? I damaged my evening dress last night and I can't go out because I haven't a thing to wear."

"Good God! What mischief did you get up to last night? Once I knew that Jim had left you at that club I knew something would happen. Why did you stay after he'd left?"

"I had to have one last fling to try and win back some of the money I'd lost. Shirl, please come and bring my grey suede suit, a blouse and some underwear. You'll find...."

"Wait a minute, love! The twins are into the fridge. No, Timmy, put that down. You mustn't throw jelly at Lisa...." The receiver clattered down at the other end of the line and the dialling tone came on to mock Teri. With a rueful grimace she replaced her receiver. Understandably Shirley had to attend to her small family before she could help any friend, but her voice had been real enough, and not at all dreamlike.

Teri ate more toast and looked around the pleasant room which was now full of sunlight and racked her memory trying to recall anything she had heard about Stephanos Nikerios's wives. Had he had two or three? And which one on the list of three had been Damien's mother? It was no use. She really knew very little about Stephanos Nikerios's marital alliances. All she knew was that he was a rags-to-riches Greek who had become a millionaire through sheer will-power and quick-wittedness.

But she should know whom Sir Arthur Wemsley had married. After all, he was a well-known businessman in England. Vaguely she remembered now her father making some comment when Sir Arthur had married for a second time. There had been a picture in the newspaper of the baronet leaving a register office with his new wife.

"So he's married the enchanting Marilyn Merrill," he had remarked.

"Sounds as if you know her," Bridget Hayton had said dryly.

"No, only of her. She used to be married to Stephanos Nikerios and I met her son when I went to see Carl Sweiss about the book he was writing on the excavations he'd done on the island of Skios.''

"Oh, I remember who she is now," Bridget had exclaimed. "She was young enough to be Nikerios's daughter. Married him for his money. Probably divorced him for money too. I wonder what she wants from Sir Arthur?''

"Perhaps she's marrying for love this time," Alex had replied in his teasing way. "And of that I'm sure *you* will approve.''

After finishing the toast Teri went to the bathroom and soon was in the bath, immersed to the shoulders in rose-scented foam. She was going to do what Damien's mother **had** done, she decided. She was going to marry him for money to solve the problem of the debt. It would keep the publishing company in the Hayton family and also the house in Richmond. She realised she would have to sink her pride and suppress her own ideals regarding love and marriage which had been passed on to her by her parents' example. It would mean bargaining with Damien when she saw him again, because there would have to be a contract between them in which certain conditions would be laid down to protect her future. Considering his back-ground and parentage the possibility of him wanting to remain married to her for ever was extremely remote.

After washing her hair and rinsing it under the shower she left the bath and towelled herself dry with a big fluffy apple green towel. Dressed again in the pyjama jacket, her nylon briefs and Lady Wemsley's dressing gown, she blew her hair dry with the blow-dryer she found in a cupboard and then wove it into two plaits which hung down over each shoulder. Returning to the bedroom, she looked round for her handbag. It wasn't anywhere she could see. Going to the bell push, she pressed it and then went over to the window to look out. Against a high thin pale blue sky fluffy clouds were tumbling before a wind and the snow on the garden lawn had almost gone. It was a bright breezy day and there was a hint of spring in the golden warmth of the sun.

"As usual Mrs. MacCracken knocked on the door before opening it and entering.

"I wondered if you'd seen my handbag," said Teri. "It's black patent leather, not very big," she made a shape with her hands, "and it has a gilt clasp."

"I've looked everywhere."

"And I haven't seen it downstairs. Perhaps you left it in Mr. Nikerios's car."

"Of course. That must be where it is." Teri felt relieved. She watched the housekeeper pick up the breakfast tray and added, "The toast and tea were very nice, thank you."

Mrs. MacCracken nodded in her approving way as she backed out of the door with the tray. As soon as she had gone Teri went over to the dressing table to survey herself in the wide mirror. Without her handbag she couldn't put on any make-up. From the mirror a slim young woman with a perfect oval face looked back at her with long-lashed dark blue eyes. The plaits made her look very young, she thought, much less than her twenty-three years. When she had been nine Damien Nikerios had been twenty-one and making a fool of himself over a woman. That meant he was much more experienced than she was in close personal relationships. David had been only six months older than herself and she had known him since childhood. If he had lived they would have been married two years by now. She might have been a mother by now. But David had been killed on his way to their wedding and she hadn't been the same since.

Teri bit hard on her lower lip and turned away to the window again, thrusting her hands into the wide sleeves of the dressing gown gripping her arms with her fingers. No handbag meant no cigarettes, no inhaled tobacco to relax her twanging nerves. She had to speak to someone. By now perhaps the twins had finished their breakfast and were playing or watching some programme on T.V. Quickly she strode to the bedside table and dialled Shirley's number. Her friend answered straight away as if she had been standing by the phone waiting for it to ring.

"Thank heaven you've phoned again!" Shirley exclaimed. "I've been trying to get you. Eventually I got the number from directory enquiries, but the woman who answered said there was no one called Miss Hayton staying there, only a Mr.... Nikerios, I think she said."

"Did the woman have a Scottish accent?" Teri asked cautiously.

"Yes, and she said she was the housekeeper. Teri, just what are you doing in that house?"

"Well, I've just had breakfast in bed," Teri began flippantly.

"Oh, all right," said Shirley with a sigh. "It's all top secret and hush-hush and you can't tell me. I recognise the signs. Lucky you, though, having breakfast in bed while I'm being run ragged by these two demons. Look, love, about your clothes, I can't possibly bring them to you today. It isn't my day for the car."

"You could come by train," suggested Teri.

"And what am I supposed to do with the twins?

Bring them with me, I suppose. Not on your life!"
growled Shirley.

"Couldn't you leave them with Mrs. Whats-her-
name next door?"

"She's out. Couldn't you borrow something to
wear from the housekeeper or from someone else
who lives there so you can travel back here and get
your clothes yourself?"

The handle of the bedroom door was turning. The
door opened and Damien appeared, carrying two big
dress boxes bearing the name of an exclusive fashion
shop. Teri watched him kick the door closed behind
him and advance towards the bed.

"Teri, are you there? Did you hear what I said?"
Shirley's voice in her ear sounded anxious.

"Yes, I heard. It's all right. I think I might be able
to do what you suggested. I have to go now. See you
later."

Teri replaced the receiver on its rest. Damien put
the boxes down on the bed and turning to her held
out her handbag.

"So it was in your car after all," she said, grasping it
eagerly and opening it at once to take out her cigarettes and lighter. "I was afraid I'd lost it." Cigarette
between her lips, she flicked the lighter.

"I would prefer it if you didn't smoke in here," he
said, his voice cold and flat. "In fact I would prefer it
if you didn't smoke at all."

Teri inhaled and let smoke trickle out from between her lips as she returned his stare. His eyes
were like black ice, she thought fancifully, and the
curl of his upper lip expressed disgust. There was
nothing warm or gentle about him this morning. He
looked what he was—a tough, bargaining Greek with
an eye to the main chance; a man it would be diffi-

cult to defeat for the simple reason that he would always avoid placing himself in a position of weakness.

"I don't smoke much," she retorted. "Only when I'm nervous."

"You're nervous now?" His peaked eyebrows went up disbelievingly while his dark glance took in the dark red robe she was wearing.

"Yes, I am. Wouldn't you be if you wakened in a strange bedroom in a strange house without any clothes?" she countered.

"You have clothes now," he replied smoothly, pointing to the two dress boxes. "I've bought you some."

"You didn't have to...."

"I know I didn't," he interrupted her with a touch of impatience. "But I wanted to, and now I'd like to see if they fit you. I took the size from the label on your evening gown."

As he stood there, his back to the sunlight streaming through the window, he seemed taller than he had last night and had a graceful length of leg she hadn't noticed before. His suit of fine English worsted was charcoal grey and well cut, the jacket fitting smoothly across his wide shoulders. Hands in his pockets, he towered over her like the prince of darkness she had imagined him to be the previous night.

"How are you feeling this morning...besides being nervous?" he asked dryly.

"Much better, thank you." Her mind was suddenly flooded with memories of his attentions of the night and to her annoyance warm blood flushed upwards from her throat to her cheeks. "It was the *ouzo* and then the wine. They were both very strong and I'm not used to strong drink." She drew on her cigarette and gave him an underbrowed glare. "I believe you wanted to make me drunk."

"Did I? Now why would I want to do that?" To her relief the coldness had gone from his voice and the ice from his eyes.

"To get me in your power."

Putting back his head, he shouted with laughter, his strong white teeth flashing in the darkness of his face.

"You're incredible," he said, shaking his head. "And have a very lively imagination. But you're quite mistaken. I didn't set out to make you drunk. I believed you to be much more hardened and experienced than you are. I had no idea the *ouzo* would have such a bad effect on you." He paused, his eyes narrowing. "Tell me, how much do you remember of what happened last night?"

"I remember feeling awfully peculiar in the restaurant and I had to get out. I thought the air might clear my head, but it didn't. Everything whirled around me and I think I bumped into something...."

"Someone," he corrected quietly. "He hit you and grabbed your handbag. I chased him and caught up with him on the next street. He spent the night in a police cell. The police want to know if you want to press charges."

"Oh," Teri felt suddenly at a disadvantage. Studying his width of shoulder and breadth of chest again, remembering the sinewy strength of his arms, she found herself sympathising with the thief he had caught. The purse snatcher must have had all the breath knocked out of him. "You must be a very fast runner," she said faintly.

"Not as fast as I used to be," he replied. "Do you remember coming here?"

"Vaguely." Her glance swerved away from his intent gaze and again colour raced up under her skin. "I remember you helped me undress and put me to bed," she whispered.

"Nothing else?" She took a last pull on her cigarette and looked round for somewhere to stub it out. Turning, Damien went over to the dressing table and brought back a small porcelain dish.

"Use this," he ordered, holding it out to her.

"I remember you got into bed with me," she said as coolly as she could, still not looking at him. "Then I went to sleep." She stubbed the cigarette out in the dish she had taken from him and looked up. The mocking glint in his eyes made her nerves quiver. "I know I went to sleep because I had a crazy dream," she blurted defensively.

"About someone called David?" he suggested, taking the dish from her and putting it down on the bedside table, then coming back to sit beside her on the edge of the bed. "Who is he?" he asked.

"He...I was going to marry him once," she said, and springing to her feet, not wanting to be near him, she walked over to the window. Now the thin film of snow had gone completely and there were puddles on the lawn and the path which glinted blue as they reflected the sky.

"He was the one who died in a car accident?" he asked.

"Yes." She stared at the garden but hardly saw it. "Why did you bring me to this house?" she queried.

"You were not well and had been hit over the head, and it was my fault. I shouldn't have let you drink the *ouzo*," he replied. "I could hardly abandon you in the middle of a London street, I had no idea where you were staying, so I brought you here, to the house where I stay when I'm in town and where I could look after you."

"You didn't have to bring me to your bedroom," she said.

"I did that because I didn't want to disturb Mrs. MacCracken to ask her to get another room ready. Also I guessed you wouldn't have wanted her to see you in the state you were in." His voice rasped dryly.

"You didn't have to sleep with me either," she went on accusingly.

"I agree—I didn't have to. But I wanted to and you asked me to stay with you, and I'm not the sort of man who can refuse an invitation like that from a woman as attractive as you are."

Teri whirled at that to glare at him across the room. Still sitting on the edge of the bed, looking thoroughly relaxed and slightly amused, hands in his trouser pockets, his legs stretched before him, he gave her one of his tantalising crooked smiles.

"It wasn't all a dream, Teri," he said softly. "It really happened. You turned to me for comfort and I comforted you, but we wanted more from each other and so...." He took his hands out of his pockets and spread them in a foreign gesture as he shrugged.

For another moment she stared at him, her mind awhirl with memories, then she swung back to the window.

"I think you are contemptible," she said coldly and clearly. "You seduced me."

"I could call you names too," he retorted, and she knew he was coming across the room to her by the nearness of his voice. "But I won't," he added, and she felt his hands on her shoulders. She flinched, twitched away from him and turned to face him. "You needn't be so upset," he murmured. "Nothing unpleasant happened. There was no seduction. You wanted to, I wanted to. It was natural and very pleasurable, something which will happen often, I hope, once we are married. You are going to marry me aren't you? You do remember saying you will?''

"I...yes, I am," she said, making her voice hard and avoiding his eyes. "But there will have to be certain conditions." She stepped past him and walked over to the bed and began to lift the lid off one of the boxes. "There'll have to be some sort of contract," she added.

Damien didn't answer and she glanced across at him. It seemed to her that he had gone rather pale, but then she dismissed the idea. In full sunlight his skin was bound to take on a lighter tone. She pushed aside the tissue paper and lifted the dress out of the box. Made of fine wool, it was very plain with a long tunic top and a knife-pleated skirt. The colour was the same dark blue of her eyes. Without thinking she took off the red dressing gown, slipped out of the pyjama jacket and unzipping the back of the dress pulled it over her head. When it was on she walked over to Damien, presenting her back to him.

"Please do up the zip," she said.

As the zip closed his knuckles brushed briefly against the nape of her neck, sending a shiver of sensuousness tingling down her spine, but ignoring the feeling, she went over to the wardrobe and with her hands on her hips surveyed herself in the long mirror.

"It's lovely," she said. "And it fits so well. Anyone would think you're accustomed to...." She broke off, frowning, a strange feeling twisting through her as she realised Damien could have gone through this scene with a woman before.

"Choosing clothes for a woman," he finished for her, at his most sardonic, and going over to the bed he took the lid off the other large box while Teri turned back to the mirror to admire the blue dress again, her eyes widening and her mouth opening a little with astonishment when she saw him appear in the mirror behind her holding a fur coat.

"Try this for size," he suggested.

She slipped her arms into the sleeves and the silken lining caressed her skin. The fur was mink, a beautiful golden brown, and the style of the coat was very contemporary, flattering her slim figure, its deep collar when turned up making a perfect frame for her pale face.

This time when Damien put his hands on her shoulders he gave her no time to flinch away from him. He spun her round and surveyed the coat critically.

"It looks well on you," he said. "But I do not care for these—what do you call them? Pigtails?" He took hold of one of the plaits and began to unweave it. "They make you look too childish, and the last thing I want is a child-wife or to be accused of cradle-snatching. What sort of conditions did you have in mind? Isn't it enough that I won't demand Alex's debt be paid if I marry you?"

Teri pulled the plait from his hand and with a few deft movements of her fingers undid it, then quickly undid the other one. She shook her head and her crinkled hair swirled about the fur collar.

"That's better," he said. "I liked the way you were wearing it last night. It made you look what you are— wayward and just a little spoilt."

"I'm not...." she began, then closed her mouth firmly. No point in getting into an argument with him. While he was talking conditions she must press her advantage. Lifting her chin, she eyed him steadily. "I have to think of the future and protect myself," she said coldly. "There might come a time when...when you decide you don't want me to be your wife any more."

Something flickered in the dark eyes, then they were veiled quickly by their lashes. His mouth twisted into a bitter grimace.

"I see," he said so quietly that she could hardly hear him. "So you're no different from the others after all." His eyelids flicked up. Ice cold, his eyes glittered devilishly. "You mean, I suppose, like father, like son," he drawled.

"Exactly," she said, and wondered vaguely why it was hurting her to deal with him in this way.

He studied her narrowly for a few seconds and then shoving his hands into his pockets moved away to lean against the dressing table.

"I think we could work something out which could be written into a contract," he said coolly. "You will receive a generous allowance while you are married to me and for as long as I'm able to provide it. In the event of a divorce," he paused and frowned, the lines around his mouth deepening cynically, then went on slowly, "I would make a settlement on you, the amount to be negotiated at the time. Are those the sort of conditions you have in mind?" She swallowed hard. It was so awful, so soul-destroying and degrading to discuss marriage with him in this way, but it had to be done. After all, it wasn't as if the marriage would be based on love, and she didn't trust him.

"*But* there are also certain conditions I shall have to insist on being included in any contract you and I sign," he added thoughtfully.

"What are they?"

"Firstly, if any child or children are born to us they

will remain in my custody should we either separate or divorce. Could you agree to that?"

"I...I...." Having a child or children hadn't been in her plan at all and she had no ready answer.

"You hadn't got as far as thinking about that," he suggested dryly.

"No, I hadn't," she admitted rather sullenly.

"Then I suggest you do think about it, because the chances that you'll have a child by me are very high. It won't be a marriage in name only, if that is what you had in mind. I shall expect you to be my wife in the fullest sense, to live where I want to live and...."

"Oh, but what about my job?" Teri put in swiftly.

"What job?"

"I work in the editorial department at Hayton's. I couldn't possibly give it up, so I'll have to live here, in London."

"No way," he replied softly. "If you're going to marry me you'll give up all idea of working and you'll live with me either in a house in Athens or at the villa I own in Skios."

"But...." she began, and broke off, biting her lip, her mind racing as she tried to find arguments to change his point of view.

"Perhaps you would like to change your mind," he suggested quietly. "But remember, if you don't agree to marry me I'll take everything Alex offered me as security."

"Why don't you try changing your mind, for once?" she countered tartly, tilting her chin at him. She could tell she was up against that stubbornness he had talked about now. She could see it in the set of his mouth and the implacable cold stare of his dark eyes.

"Once I've decided on a course of action I never change," he replied calmly.

"Not even if that course of action leads to disaster?" she queried, and to her surprise he laughed.

"You are too serious," he said. "Our marriage won't lead to disaster. But you haven't answered my question. Do you want to back out? Shall I go to your father's solicitors today and tell them that I want the ownership of that house and the shares transferred from Alex's name to mine?"

"Do I have to answer now?" she asked in a last-minute stand.

"Yes."

Once more her mind flicked over alternatives quickly and she rejected them all as useless.

"No, I don't want to back out," she replied, recklessly burning her boats as usual, taking a gamble, confident that she would be able to find a way round the conditions he wanted to impose eventually. There were ways and means of avoiding having children. He would grow tired of having her living with him all the time and then she would be able to return to work at Hayton's. The main thing now was to get him to sign a contract in which he would give up all claim to the security her father had offered him. "How soon can we do it?" she added.

"The sooner the better for all concerned, is that what you're thinking?" Damien asked with that uncanny knack he had for guessing what she had in mind. "Shall we say a week from today? That should give the lawyers time to draw up the contract and give us time to get a special licence. Agreed?"

"Agreed," she nodded.

"You'll want to get in touch with your mother, I expect. Maybe you'd like her to be present at the ceremony."

"No. I think it would be best if she doesn't know

about it until after we're married," she muttered, and before he could question her she added quickly, "Will you ask any of your family to attend?"

"My father is too old and infirm to travel these days and my mother won't be back in England. I propose that after the marriage is legalised we go to Skios and stay there for a while so that you can meet my father and some of my relatives." Damien began to move towards the door. "It's almost time for lunch," he said. "Perhaps when you have finished dressing you'll come downstairs and we'll go out. After eating we'll go and see the lawyers about that contract."

He opened the door and went out, closing it behind him. Alone, Teri sank down on the edge of the bed, feeling a sudden rush of weariness set in. She had done it. She had bargained with him and had got him to agree to some conditions. She should be feeling triumphant, pleased with herself, but instead she felt a strange sense of loss. What she had lost she wasn't quite sure. There was just this niggling feeling that in some way she had gone down in the estimation of Damien Nikerios.

CHAPTER THREE

OUT of a wine-dark sea, against a sky streaked crimson and gold by the setting sun, the island of Skios loomed black and mysterious. As she stood on the bow of Stephanos Nikerios's motor yacht, listening to the surge of water beneath the sleek white hull, Teri held herself taut and straight and no one could guess from the cool composure of her pale face at the emotions which were churning through her at that moment.

Earlier that day she had deliberately changed the course of her life by signing a contract which had made her the wife of a rich and powerful man, and now she was on her way to meet another rich and powerful man. Her hands tensed on the rail in front of her and the thick gold band on the third finger of her left hand shone with a dull opulence as it caught the rays of the setting sun. She stared at it, feeling a sort of pain quiver through her. What had she done? She had become Damien's wife in a short civil ceremony and as a result had broken with all she had ever known, had left country and friends and above all had cut the bonds of kinship.

Teri's mouth trembled and her hands clenched even more on the rail as she recalled her mother's reaction to her marriage. After the ceremony this morning she had phoned Bridget immediately, from Wemsley House, where she and Damien had called

on their way to Heathrow to pick up his luggage, and
had explained what she had done and why she had
done it.

"You should have told me before!" Bridget had exclaimed. "Why didn't you?"

"Because I know you would have tried to stop
me," Teri had replied. "And then he would have
taken everything, the house and Hayton's. I couldn't
let him do that to you and to Dick, I couldn't!"

"But I'm sure there must have been some other
way," Bridget had said.

"There wasn't. It was a case of either marry him or
lose everything. He was quite adamant about it."

"But to marry a man like him, whom you hardly
know, in cold blood! How could you, Teri?"

"It wasn't easy, but I've done it now. We've signed
a contract, so I'm protected for the future."

"Oh, no!" Bridget had groaned. "That's just what
that awful woman, his mother, did when she married
Stephanos Nikerios. She was a night-club singer and
not a very good one at that. Teri... don't you see, to
do what she did and what you have done is like selling
yourself. What would your father have thought?"

"It was he who got us into the mess in the first
place. If he'd been better at business and..." Teri had
broken off suddenly, realising she had been about to
criticise her beloved father. "Oh, Mum," she had
added gently, "please try to understand and not feel
too badly about it. I did it for you and Dick and it will
turn out all right, I promise it will. I've written to you
about it and so has Mr. Fenton, Dad's solicitor, to tell
you the debt to Damien is cancelled by my marriage
to him. I have to go now. We're flying to Greece, to
stay on the island of Skios. Perhaps when you've got
over the shock of having Stephanos Nikerios's son

and heir for a son-in-law you'll come out and join me there for a holiday. Damien says it's a lovely peaceful place. He has his own villa there, near to his father's and...."

"No, never!" Bridget's voice came over the line quite strongly.

"What do you mean?" Teri had demanded hastily, aware that Damien had come into the room behind her and was telling her impatiently to hurry up or they would miss the plane.

"I'll never come to visit you," Bridget had gone on, her voice rising agitatedly. "I don't want to meet Damien Nikerios or his father. Nor do I want to see you while you're married to a man like that. Oh, Teri," Bridget's voice had broken suddenly, "when I think of how you were with David, how you loved him...how could you do this? How could you marry for money and not for love?"

"I don't know, but I have," Teri had replied, her voice hard, revealing nothing of the hurt which had been searing her. "I can't talk any more. We're leaving now. Goodbye, Mother, and please...please try to understand."

Damien hadn't asked her how her mother had taken the news of their marriage and she hadn't told him. In fact they had talked very little on the flight. She had been too numb with the pain her mother had inflicted on her and he had been cool and remote as if he too had been coping with some inner conflict. Only when they had at last reached Athens and they had been driving through the streets on the way to the port of Piraeus had she come alive for the first time that day, excited by glimpses of the Acropolis on the Sacred Rock, its marble columns shimmering like gold in the sunlight.

The rumble of the yacht's engines slowed down. Looking up, she saw the boat was nosing its way between navigational buoys on which red and white lights glittered, and entering a small harbour. All colour had gone from the sky now and in the brief twilight the water shimmered pale lavender, surrounded on three sides by dark hills. The round tower and thatched pointed roof of a windmill appeared silhouetted against the soft dusky blue of the evening sky and then was hidden from view by the crumbling walls of an old fort as the yacht slid smoothly past a group of multi-coloured fishing boats, its wash making them rock gently. Buildings, all cube-shaped, crowded along the edge of the wharfs and zigzagged up the hillsides in a series of terraces, walls gleaming softly white and grey as they caught the last of the daylight.

The yacht sidled into its berth, warps were thrown and caught, jokes and shouts were exchanged between the men on the yacht and those on the wharf. Damien appeared and came towards her and she felt as always that faint prickling of skin and rising of hairs on her neck that his physical presence caused. Resentment because he could affect her in such a way made her turn her back deliberately on him and begin to walk away. During the past week his behaviour had been puzzling. Cold and aloof, he had kept his distance from her and there had been a number of times when she had wondered if he would change his mind about marrying her, had half expected, even this morning, for Mr. Fenton to tell her that Mr. Nikerios had decided not to sign the contract but would prefer to keep to the original agreement he had had with her father.

"Are you ready to go ashore now?" he asked behind her. Teri turned and nodded. "This way, then," he murmured, bending his head to peer at her closely. "You're very pale. Are you tired?"

"I'm always pale," she retorted as they walked towards the gangway which had been put in place. "Mmm, what a lovely smell! Pines, I think, but other scents too. What else grows on the island?"

"Olives, figs, eucalyptus, orange and lemon trees, grapes, wild flowers by the millions," he replied indifferently, and went before her along the gangway, turning when he reached the wharf to steady her as she stepped down.

There was light shafting out of windows on the wharf and music and laughter coming from the open door of a *taverna*. People were leaning out of other windows watching what was going on and a man's voice shouted something as Damien guided her towards an open horse-drawn carriage. He paused, tilted back his head and called back an answer. At once there were shrieks of delight and some hand-clapping and several voices, many of them belonging to women who called out more remarks.

"What's going on?" Teri asked, wishing she could understand Greek.

"They wanted to know who the woman in the silver wig is," he replied, amusement warming his voice as he helped her to step up into the carriage. "I told them we were married today and so they are offering their congratulations and welcome to you."

"I didn't realize there would be other people on the island," she said. "I thought your father owned it."

"He does, but buying it didn't give him the right to turn off the people whose families have always lived here," he replied as he took his place beside her. He gave a crisp order to the driver and the carriage began to move forward. "There are no cars on the island. Traffic is restricted to motor-bikes, occasional delivery trucks and a bus service and these carriages. But since distances are short it is possible to walk almost everywhere if you have the time," he added. "Are you warm enough?"

"Yes, thank you."

Leaving the waterfront, the road which the carriage followed wound close to the shoreline, beneath the overhanging branches of pine trees. Sand shimmered with silvery light and there were glints of bluish-green phosphorescence in the dark water rippling at the edge of the sand. Overhead the stars twinkled in a sky which was rapidly changing from violet grey to deep royal blue. Night had come to Skios swiftly and silently.

Damien's hand, large and warm, closed suddenly over Teri's hand which was resting casually on her knee.

"You don't feel warm," he murmured, moving closer to her and putting his other arm along the back of the leather-covered carriage seat behind her shoulders. "But perhaps your skin is always cool, just as it is always pale," he added mockingly.

It was the first time he had touched her since he had made love to her that night over a week ago when, with slow expert caresses, he had inflamed hidden potent nerves in her body until it had melted with passion. Now the gentle seductive movement of his thumb against the delicate skin over her wrist sent a delicious tingle tripping up her arm. It flickered like a flame along her nerves, spreading dangerously and setting off a series of small explosions somewhere near the pit of her stomach.

Afraid of her own passionate nature, afraid it might overcome the cool direction of her mind, Teri curled her hand into a fist, pointed nails digging into the palm as she exercised control and gradually slid her hand from under his. To her dismay his hand didn't move from her knee but stayed where it was, long fingers tightening slightly and suggestively, sending new and different tingles skipping along different nerves.

At once she moved her leg, to cross the knee over the other one, and his hand slipped away but, just as she was letting out a quiet sigh of relief, the fingers of his other hand, the one behind her back, began to play among the coils of hair which covered the nape of her neck. With a quick jerk of her head and shoulders, she shifted along the seat, right into the corner, keeping her face averted from him, looking out at the dark glinting mass of water.

"It's a lovely night," she said coolly. "Is it always as mild as this at this time of the year?"

"The temperature varies, I guess, between fifty and seventy degrees in the month of April. Out here, on the island, it is of course cooler than it would be in Athens this evening," he replied smoothly.

"I noticed the ruins of an old building as we entered the harbour," she went on.

"The remains of an old fortress. Skios had its moment of glory in the mid-eighteenth century when it sent a fleet of sailing ships to trade in the Mediterranean. You'll find that many of the old mansions, including my father's house, have an Italianate look— that's because the sea captains and ship-owners had them built by Venetian craftsmen whom they brought here." He paused, then added dryly. "I hadn't reckoned on having to act as a tourist guide. Is there anything else you would like to know?"

Teri didn't answer. This was the beginning, she

thought, the beginning of their marriage, and as it began so would it continue. Somehow tonight she had to make it clear to him that just because he had married her he couldn't take her when he felt like it. She had to keep him at a distance. Whenever he touched her she must move away, show no response at all, and gradually he would leave her alone, go his own way, probably turn to other women. And when he did that she would have an excuse to divorce him, about a year from now....

"*Ouch*!" Her cry of pain was involuntary as he took hold of some of her hair and pulled it sharply. She turned her head to protest and he moved in quickly, pushing a heavy thigh across hers and pressing it down against the seat until she felt a broken spring jab into her. With his free hand he gripped her chin so that she couldn't avoid the lips which swooped down to hers.

His kiss was a flagrant act of possession, a blistering insult which roused all her feminism. She wanted to fight him off, to hit him with her fists or scratch at his cheeks with her nails. But some instinct warned her that to react in such a way would only rouse his temper and bring some sort of fierce retaliation, so she kept still, neither reacting nor responding, and slowly his lips softened and gradually he withdrew them from hers.

"What's the matter?" he asked softly, but he didn't move away and she could feel his breath on her cheek.

"Nothing," she replied coldly.

"I don't believe you." His fingers released her chin and she felt his knuckles brush gently along her jaw in a tantalisingly tender caress which caused her to bite her lip sharply. "You're pale, you're cold and you've hardly said a word all day."

"You haven't been exactly chatty yourself," she taunted.

"That's because I've had a lot on my mind," he said, and to her relief he moved away from her.

"Business problems?" she asked, shifting warily out of the corner, off the broken spring.

"Yes." He paused, then added quietly, "I'll probably have to go to New York tomorrow. I should have gone today, but I had promised I would bring you here to meet my father. Will you mind staying here for a few days by yourself? I can assure you, you'll be well looked after by Tina, my housekeeper. I should be back on Friday."

"You're sure you don't want me to come to New York with you?" she asked politely.

"Do you want to come?" he asked, surprise lilting in his voice.

"Not really."

"I thought that would be the way of it," he replied enigmatically.

The hooves of the horse clip-clopped on the stony surface of the road, the waves shushed softly on the sand and a light wind sighed in the branches of the pines. But in the back of the carriage there was silence, the brittle edgy silence between two people who were caught up in an age-old battle, the battle of the sexes.

The driver of the carriage said something to the horse and the carriage turned up a driveway. Lights twinkled and the square shape of a white house loomed out of the trees. The carriage stopped in front of three arches, illuminated underneath by lamps hanging in brackets.

A door opened and more light spilled out into the pine-scented darkness. A woman's voice called out something in Greek and Damien called back an answer as he helped Teri down from the carriage and urged her towards the door.

"This is Tina." he said to Teri, then spoke quickly to the woman in Greek.

Teri was aware of being assessed curiously by a pair of sharp black eyes set under a low forehead. Braided black hair was swept back severely from a widow's peak and knotted at the nape. The woman was short and sturdy-looking. She nodded at Teri and spoke to her.

"What shall I say to her?" Teri demanded, turning to Damien. "Oh, please tell me something I can say to her in Greek."

"For now, all you need to say is *kalispera*—it means good evening," he said.

Teri repeated the word slowly and watched the woman's thick-lipped mouth curve upwards at the corners in a slight smile.

"Good evening, Mrs. Nikerios," Tina replied in heavily accented English. "And welcome to Skios. Will you enter now?"

"You speak English well," exclaimed Teri.

"Of course she does. She lived for a while in the States," said Damien with a touch of impatience. "Is Arnie about, Tina?"

"Yes. He is in the kitchen," replied the woman.

"I'll go and fetch him to help me with the luggage while you show Mrs. Nikerios to her room. I expect she'll want to wash and change after the journey."

He walked away down a passageway, his footsteps echoing on the mosaic tiles.

"This way, please," Tina said to Teri, and led the way in the opposite direction, between rough white walls which on one side were broken by archways opening on to a shadowy courtyard and on the other by doorways. The room into which Tina led her was square and simple and had one window. Its furnishings were also simple and unpretentious but of the highest quality. Sea colours, green and blues, were blended together in the plain curtains and bedcovers and the stone floor had been covered with a thick sea-green carpet.

"This is the bathroom," said Tina, opening one of two doors.

"And the other door?" asked Teri, beginning to slip off the jacket of her suede suit.

"That leads to another bedroom," replied Tina stonily. There was no evidence of the smile now. From beneath her heavy eyebrows her black eyes studied Teri with a certain hostility which was chilling. Just then the half-open door was pushed open further and a short wiry man came in, carrying Teri's luggage. He put it down at the end of the bed and straightening up he too stared at her, his twinkling grey eyes roving over her with interest.

"This is Arnie, my husband," Tina said stiffly.

"*Kalispera*," Teri said slowly, and to her surprise the man laughed at her.

"No need to waste your efforts on me, missus," he said in a cockney-accented English. "I'm from the U.K. like yourself. Pleased to meetcha." He moved to the door and as he went by her Teri noticed a certain rolling swagger to his stride as if he had spent much time on a ship, and below the edge of the short sleeves of his white shirt she glimpsed the bluish marks of an intricate tattoo mark.

"You want me to stay and help you unpack?" Tina asked, backing towards the door, and noticing that hostility again Teri declined. The woman went out

and the door closed. Feeling as if she had been suddenly released from some sort of constraint, Teri un-
buttoned the jacket of her grey suede suit, took it off
and threw it across the bed, looking about the room as
she did so, her glance coming to rest on the door
which Tina had said led to another bedroom.

The man called Arnie had brought only one lot of
luggage. Had Damien's been taken into that other
room? She hoped so, because separate bedrooms
were just what she wanted. Going over to the door,
she turned the knob and pushed. The door remained
solidly closed. It appeared to be locked. From the
other side?

Teri soon unpacked all her clothes and when they
were hung in the closet provided, she undressed completely and wrapped herself in a long clinging robe of
blue chenille. Like the bedroom, the bathroom was
very simple, but the hot water was almost boiling and
it wasn't long before the room was wrathed with
steam and she was relaxing in the bath.

She was lying full length under the clear water
when the door opened abruptly and Damien walked
in. Without his shirt, the olive-tinted skin of his bare
shoulders gleaming silkily under the electric light, he
stood with one hand on his hips and the other one on
the doorknob looking down at her.

"I don't want to hurry you too much, but we're
expected at my father's house in exactly twenty minutes and I'd like a wash too before I go," he said.

"Oh." Water swirled and swished noisily, some of
it slopping over the edge of the bath as she jack-knifed
into a sitting position, covering her breasts with her
arms in an instinctive protective movement.

"Couldn't you use your own bathroom?" she quavered.

"This is my bathroom," he replied. "Come on, out you get. You've been in long enough. I'll help you dry, if you like."

"No...no...go away. Oh, how dare you walk in here without knocking first!" she flared, glaring at him through the steam. "Have you no manners?"

"A few, but I wasn't brought up to be a gentleman," he replied easily. "With a father who was born and grew up in severe poverty and spent his early life as an able seaman in a small freighter and a mother who used to earn her living belting out songs in sleazy New York waterfront joints I didn't have much opportunity to learn much etiquette. Here, give me your hand and I'll help you out. Unless" his eyes gleamed mockingly and his mouth curved satirically "unless you'd like me to join you in there. Making love in the bath can be an interesting but slippery affair."

"No!" Teri shouted the word at him and got to her feet quickly, intending to leap out and at the same time grab the big towel she had put handily on the bathroom stool, but one of her feet slipped on the wet smoothness of porcelain surface of the bath and she fell forward right into Damien's arms.

"Mmmm, you smell delicious," he murmured, his lips searing her throat while his hands slipped down over her bare back to curve about her buttocks. "I wish—" he added, and broke off, sliding his hands up to her waist to push her away from him. His eyelids drifted down over the darkness of his eyes as his glance went to the tilted-up pink tips of her breasts. "This is the first time I've seen you properly," he whispered. "And I'm tempted, oh, so very tempted...." His dark head tipped forward and Teri moved swiftly, instinctively backwards, groped for and found the towel and thrust it between them, covering her breasts with it. Across the small space which separated them their glances met and locked, his narrowed with amusement, hers wide and wary.

"Anyone would think we hadn't been lovers," he said.

"We haven't," she retorted.

"But the first time we met...."

"I prefer to forget the first time we met," she said coldly. "Excuse me. The bath is all yours. I'll dry in the bedroom," she added, and stepped by him into the bedroom, closing the door behind her.

By the time Damien emerged from the bathroom, his hair curling damply about his forehead, his skin smelling of the same lavender-scented soap that she had used, she was fully dressed, wearing the dress of fine blue wool he had given her, and was standing at the window, looking out and smoking.

"I have told you before I wish you wouldn't smoke in my bedroom," he said sharply, coming across to her and taking the half-smoked cigarette from between her fingers.

"Your bedroom?" she exclaimed. "But I thought...." Her glance went to the other door which was slightly open. "Tina said there was another bedroom through there," she added weakly.

"There is, a small one, with a single bed suitable for a child to sleep in. I use it as a dressing room only," he said coolly, going over to the chest of drawers and stubbing the cigarette in a small glass dish. "I sleep in here." He swung round to look at her. "You're nervous again. Why?" he asked. "Is it because you'll have to share a bed with me tonight?"

Teri opened her mouth to answer him, changed her mind, shook her head negatively and turned away to look out of the window again. There wasn't really much to see, just the soft blue-black sky above the black outline of trees and a few stars winking wickedly at her.

"I think that...Tina doesn't like me," she muttered.

"That matters?" He sounded surprised.

"Well, yes, it does, since I'm going to stay here for the next few days."

"I wouldn't worry about it. Tina will soon come round. At the moment she's jealous."

"Jealous? Why?" She whirled to look at him. He had pulled on a clean shirt, a leisure shirt of pale cream linen with short sleeves and a deeply V'd neckline, and was standing in the doorway of the other room, undoing the belt which held up his suit trousers in preparation for taking them off. "Surely you haven't...she doesn't...." She broke off, horrified at the idea of him ever having had an affair with a woman who was obviously about twenty years older than he was. But then considering his background heaven knew what sort of women he had had affairs with.

"Tina had a great affection for me, yes," he replied, laughter lilting in his voice. "For a while, when I was an infant living where I was born in the States, she was my nursemaid, and she is always jealous of any other woman I look at, even of my mother. Several years ago at the time I decided I needed my own house here on Skios I wrote to her asking her if she would like the job of looking after it. By that time she was married to Arnie, who had been in the British Merchant Navy. They both saw coming here as a chance of being able to live and work together at last." He lifted his shoulders in a shrug. "So far it has worked out very well."

He turned back into the smaller room and pushed the door to. When he appeared again he was wearing cream linen slacks to match his shirt and a dark brown blazer. His glance flicked over her.

"I suggest you take a jacket or cardigan to wear as we are going to walk. Sometimes the wind off the sea is cool at night," he said. "Ready?"

As they walked along a well-defined path through the pines a path which zigzagged higher and higher Damien kept her arm threaded through his and Teri made no attempt to pull free because not knowing the way she needed his guidance. She needed his strength and self-confidence to support her through the forthcoming meeting with Stephanos Nikerios, because she had to admit she was nervous.

During the past week, while she had been preparing to marry Damien, she had managed to find out more about his father. It seemed that Stephanos's first wife had died suddenly, leaving him with two grown daughters and no son when he was almost fifty years of age. Soon afterwards he had had a heart attack and as a result had panicked and had rushed into marriage with Marilyn Merrill, an American night club singer on whom he had fathered a son during a brief affair he had had with her two years earlier. He had married her in order to legitimise Damien's birth and so that he would have an heir to his millions, should he die suddenly. Later he and Marilyn had agreed to separate and Damien had been left in his custody.

But he hadn't had another heart attack and he hadn't died, and now at eighty-two he left most of the organising of his considerable shipping business and other financial investments to Damien and spent most of his time in the big sprawling villa, the lights of which Teri could now see twinkling through the trees, in the company of his third wife, Melina.

The house was built on the same traditional lines as Damien's villa, but the arches which concealed the main entrance were finer and had a Venetian touch, as Damien had said. Inside wide passages ran round all four sides of a central courtyard. As at the other villa the atmosphere was one of simplicity both in the furnishings and the decoration, but the signs of wealth were there, showing in the numerous original paintings hanging on the walls, in the thickness and quality of the carpets and in the handsome hand-made teak furniture of the room into which Damien led the way.

There were three people in the room, but Teri noticed only one of them, an old man sitting in a wheelchair. It was easy to recognise Stephanos Nikerios from the occasional photograph she had seen of him in magazines and newspapers and also from a certain likeness to Damien. There were the same strangely peaked black eyebrows giving the face a satanic appearance, the bold downward curving nose, the almost black, enigmatical eyes. But Stephanos's sparse hair was straight and entirely grey, the curve of his mouth lacked the humour of Damien's. There was a certain coarseness about him which showed also in his voice when, seeing them, he raised it and shouted something across the room in Greek which Damien answered in the same language, causing one of the other people in the room to laugh.

"What did he say?" demanded Teri in an urgent whisper, pulling on Damien's arm. "Tell me what he said!" She didn't like not knowing the language. It put her at a disadvantage. She must make an effort to learn it while she stayed here; otherwise she would miss too much that was going on.

"He says we're exactly five minutes late. He's a great stickler for punctuality, hates to be kept waiting," he murmured, urging her across the wide room towards the old man who was staring at her assessingly. Behind him a woman was standing, one hand resting lightly on his shoulder. She was another black-haired, black-eyed Greek, with a dusky gold skin, and on her fingers and around her neck emeralds and diamonds glittered with cold sparks.

"And what did you say to him? What made someone laugh?" asked Teri out of the corner of her mouth. The woman was staring at her with a sort of incredulity.

"I'm not going to tell you," said Damien. "I've a feeling you might take offence and turn on your heel and walk out on me."

"Oh!" She was so surprised by his answer she couldn't think of anything to say, and then they were in front of the old man and Damien was introducing her and Stephanos was looking up at her from under his beetling brows, giving her an insolent appraising glance which made her hands curl at her sides and tilt her chin at him defiantly.

"So you're Alex Hayton's daughter, are you?" growled Stephanos in heavily accented English, and again Teri was surprised. "Are you a gambler like him? You must be if you've taken on this cub of mine. Think you can tame him?"

"I'm not sure that I want to tame him," retorted Teri. "I hadn't realised you knew my father," she added, sinking on to a chair which had been placed conveniently near the wheelchair, aware that Damien and the dark woman had moved away slightly and were talking quietly, almost intimately to one another, their heads close together.

"I met him once, years ago." The sharp black eyes appraised her again. "You've a look of him about you." His mouth curved in a leering smile. "I suppose you wouldn't like to give an old man a kiss? Time was, when I was younger, like this guy here," he jerked a thumb in Damien's direction, "all the girls wanted to kiss me—but I was handsome then, and strong. Now I'm only a bag of bones, most of them arthritic."

"But you're still handsome," said Teri, and leaning forward put her soft lips to his thin cheek, her nervousness leaving her suddenly as she realised that though once he had been a tough, go-getting business tycoon he was now only a lonely old man. "I hope...." she began, and broke off, seeing out of the corner of her eye the dark woman link her arm through Damien's. Slowly they walked away to another part of the room. Something hot and sharp seemed to twist through Teri's breast and she experienced an overwhelming urge to spring to her feet and go after Damien, to pull him away from the woman.

It took all of her self-control to remain where she was and to drag her gaze away from them back to Stephanos' face. The black eyes were watching her narrowly.

"That's Melina, my third wife," he said abruptly. "Nice-looking woman, isn't she? Since I've been confined to this..." he hit the arm of the wheelchair with the flat of his hand, "I've had to have someone to look after me, a nurse. I didn't want a male nurse, so my daughter found Melina for me. It seemed convenient to marry her and shut up those blasted gossip-mongers. So you think I'm handsome, eh?" he grinned at her, showing that he still had most of his teeth. "Now let me return the compliment. You're beautiful in your Anglo-Saxon way. 'Angels, not Angles'—didn't someone say that once?" He chuckled and then raising his voice called out, "Hey, Paul, get over here! Come and meet my daughter-in-law." He leaned forward and whispered wickedly, "If you think I'm handsome, wait until you see this fellow, my grandson Paul Turner. Like Damien, he's part-American. My eldest daughter Cassie married Tom Turner who now runs our New York office."

The young man who approached them was indeed handsome, like the pictures Teri had seen in books of statues of Adonis. He had the straight forehead, the straight nose, the perfectly moulded full-lipped mouth, the rounded cleft chin. Healthily tanned, his skin had the sheen of bronze. Bronze-coloured too were the tight curls which clung closely to his well-shaped head. Under finely arched bronzed eyebrows his eyes were a deep indigo blue in striking contrast with the rest of his colouring. He was casually dressed in dark blue slacks and a round-necked short-sleeved cotton shirt.

There was an almost sullen discontented droop to his mouth which disappeared when he smiled at Teri to show perfectly even white teeth.

"Hi," he said, shaking her hand. "Nice to see someone around my own age. I've only been here a few days and already I'm bored out of my mind." He glanced sideways at Stephanos, who was propelling his wheelchair towards the shadowy corner where Damien and Melina were talking. "I hope grandfather didn't hear me," he said. "He's been really great to me, letting me stay." He looked back at her, his mouth twisting wryly. "I guess I should explain. I'm a fugitive at the moment from parental displeasure. I got into a mess at my university, had to drop out just before my final exams and flee the country. The only place I could think of coming was here. Grandfather is going to get me a place on one of his freighters as a deck hand. He says it didn't do him or Damien any harm, going to sea." He paused and gave her another twisted grin. "I'm sure running on about myself, aren't I? It's because there's been no one here for me to talk to. Grandfather gets tired, Melina doesn't speak English or understand it. How long are you and Damien going to stay?"

"I'm not sure. I'll be here at least for the next week. He's going to New York tomorrow and will be back Friday, he says."

"Oh, yeah. He's going to help sort out the jam my father has got into with some labour union over there. He's a great guy, is Damien. Cool as they come on the surface, but touch him where it hurts and you find there's a lot of hot Greek fire smouldering underneath. It flares up suddenly and before you know it you've been scorched." His glance flicked over her. "You look a little different from the usual woman he associates with. How come you've married him? Can't be for love, so it must be for money."

"What makes you think that?" Teri parried.

"A certain cynicism, developed through being a member of a wealthy family. We're always suspicious of anyone who flatters us or makes up to us, can never believe they like us for ourselves," he drawled.

Teri looked away from him towards the others. They were coming across the room. The woman Melina was pushing the wheelchair now, her eyelids covering her eyes, her face impassive.

"Teri, I'd like you to meet Melina." Damien's voice was cool, impersonal. "She doesn't speak English, so greet her in Greek, will you, the way I told you to speak to Tina?''

Teri spoke the greeting quietly and Melina looked up. No smile lit up her face. She merely nodded her head and whispered the same greeting, then looked down again at her hands resting on the back of the armchair.

''I'm going to take Damien away from you for a while, my dear,'' said Stephanos. ''There are matters of business we must discuss before he goes off to New York. But I'll see you again tomorrow. Come up here any time you like. Use the swimming pool.'' He glanced across at Paul, a mocking twinkle in his eye. ''You'll look after her, won't you, lad?''

''I'll be glad to, Grandfather,'' Paul replied. ''Goodnight.''

''I won't be too long, perhaps an hour,'' Damien murmured to Teri as he came round to her side.

''I might go back to the other house,'' she said coolly. ''It's been a long day and I'd like to go to bed.''

His eyebrows drew together in a frown, his eyes glinted and his mouth tightened. For a moment she thought some of the Greek fire Paul had talked about was going to flare up and scorch her. Then his eyelids dropped over his eyes and he lifted his shoulders in a shrug.

''As you wish,'' he said, and turned to Paul. ''Like to do something for me? Like to escort Teri back to my villa? She isn't sure of the way yet.''

''It'll be a pleasure,'' said Paul gallantly, giving Teri an outrageous wink.

''I'll see you later,'' Damien whispered, putting his arm about Teri and bending his head to kiss her temple. ''Wait up for me,'' he added softly, and made no attempt to hide his passion. It was there adding a fiery glow to the darkness of his eyes, a sensual curve to his slightly parted lips and a bruising strength to the fingers which curved about her waist.

"I'll try," she said, slipping out of his grasp, and patting back a yawn with the back of her hand. "But I'm not promising anything."

"Damien!" Stephanos's voice shouted back to them from the passage, harsh and hectoring. Damien gave her one more flaming look, then turning on his heel he strode out of the room.

"Want to go now?" Paul asked, and Teri turned to glance at him. He was watching her too, as Stephanos had earlier.

"Yes, but you don't have to come. I'm sure I can find my own way. It isn't far."

She began to move towards the archway which led out into the passage.

"I'll come with you anyway," said Paul, falling into step beside her. "I like to walk at night on the island and listen to its ghosts. Have you ever been to Greece before?"

"No, I haven't. I'm looking forward to visiting some of the well-known sites."

"Too bad Damien has to go away," he replied as they went through the front door. "But I'll be glad to go with you to any place you want to see, show you around. Right here in Skios there are the remains of a palace built in the Mycenean Age. It was discovered and excavated by Carl Zweiss, the German archaeologist. I expect you've heard of him."

"Our company...I mean...Hayton's published the book he wrote about it. I'd like to visit it. Could we go tomorrow?"

"Sure we could." His voice was enthusiastic and she felt his hand under her elbow. "We go this way, not that. You see, it's a good thing I came with you," he chided softly. "You'd have taken the wrong path through the trees, Aunt Teri."

"Now why do you call me Aunt?" she exclaimed laughingly.

"Damien is my uncle, or rather my half-uncle, to be precise. You're married to him, so that makes you my half-aunt."

"But you don't call him Uncle Damien."

"That's true, I don't."

"Then don't you dare call me Aunt Teri! I won't have anything to do with you if you do."

"Okay, I won't ... Teri." His hand slipped down her arm and he linked her fingers in hers. "I could get to like you a lot," he murmured. "I sense you're one of those independent women who likes to lead her own life and who doesn't pose a threat to any man with whom she becomes involved. Could be that's why Damien has chosen you. He's always been as wary as a cat and likes to walk by himself." He paused, then added, "I was right, wasn't I? You have married him for his money."

"Perhaps." She untwined her fingers from his.

"A wife by contract, eh?" he jeered. "Like his mother was. Have you met Marilyn yet?"

"No. Is there something wrong in signing a contract when you marry?" she retorted. "It seems to me more people who marry are doing it these days. It saves a lot of argument and unpleasantness if the marriage doesn't work out."

"I guess so. But I wouldn't have thought you would take that line. You strike me as being a romantic at heart, doing all for love and that sort of thing."

"Could be my romantic days are over," she replied lightly.

"Which means you have been in love," Paul probed delicately. "What happened? Did the man you loved let you down?"

"He died," she said flatly, and hurried ahead of him. "Do you mind if we talk about something else? Can you speak Greek?"

"I can. Learnt it at my mother's knee," he replied mockingly.

"Could you teach me some...while you're here, I mean? If Damien is going to be away a lot, I'll need to know it, for everyday purposes...."

"And so that you'll know what the rest of us are saying about you, I suppose," he said shrewdly. "Made you feel at a disadvantage back there just now, didn't it, not knowing what Damien was saying to Melina and what she was saying to him?"

Teri froze in her tracks and turned to him. In the light twinkling up from Damien's villa she could see the outline of his shoulders and chest in the pale cotton shirt, the faint sheen of skin taut across one cheekbone, the glint of the whites of his eyes.

"You're very observant," she remarked.

"Trained to be," he murmured. "Especially where people are concerned. I was studying to be a psychiatrist before I dropped out of university. Watching people, and trying to analyse their motives, is what I like doing most. You're right to be wary of Melina. If looks could kill you you'd be dead now, judging by the look she gave you when you first appeared tonight."

"But why? Why should she react to me like that? We've never met and I haven't done anything to hurt her."

"Oh, yes, you have. You've married Damien, which is something she would have liked to have done. All the family knows that it was him she hoped to catch as a husband when she came here to be Grandfather's nurse. But Damien is a pretty hard person to catch and she got tired of waiting, so when Stephanos proposed to her she accepted, thinking, I guess, that a bird in the hand...well, you know the old saying. But she still wants Damien." Again he paused and then added slowly, "I wouldn't be at all surprised if she does her best to delay Damien tonight after he's finished talking to Grandfather, and I'm willing to bet it'll be the early hours of the morning before he returns to his villa."

Teri said nothing, and turning, continued along the path. Paul caught up with her and in silence they descended to the garden of the villa. At the three arches over the entrance they both stopped.

"I hope I haven't said anything to upset you," Paul said softly, moving closer to her.

"No, not at all. As you've pointed out, I'm a wife by contract. That means Damien and I have agreed to continue to lead our own lives. If he wants to stay up half the night talking to Melina that's his affair, not mine. Thanks for walking and talking with me. What time shall I see you tomorrow?"

"Not too early," he replied, his teeth flashing as he grinned. "Do you like to swim?"

"I do. But will it be warm enough?"

"If it isn't the water in Grandfather's pool can always be heated. Afterwards we could walk over to the site of the palace and I can tell you more gruesome stories about the love life of the Nikerios family."

"All right. Will eleven be too early for you?"

"I'll be at the poolside waiting for you." He reached out and grasped one of her hands and raised it to his lips in a courtly gesture, murmuring something in Greek. "That means goodnight, mistress, and sleep well. Now say this after me: *ka-lee-neekh-ta sas.*" He spoke the words slowly and phonetically.

"What does it mean?" she asked.

"Goodnight."

Teri said the word, putting the emphasis on the third syllable as he had done.

"Good," he nodded. "First lesson over. We'll do more tomorrow when we're up at the palace."

Inside the villa was quiet. An oil lamp burned steadily on a small table in the entrance hall, casting dark shadows over the white walls. Another lamp illuminated the passageway along which Teri tiptoed towards the bedroom. She took her time preparing for bed, and for a while lay reading the Agatha Christie novel she had brought with her. But for once the skilful weaving of the plot did not hold her attention. Her mind kept wandering over the day's events and she kept seeing superimposed on the page before her an image of Damien talking to Melina.

Abruptly she slammed the book closed, put it down, switched off the light and settled herself for sleep. So what did it matter if Damien and Melina were having an affair? It made no difference to her. She didn't care if he didn't come to this bed tonight. In fact she didn't want him to come. She didn't want him, it was as simple as that.

Some time later, she still wasn't asleep. Fumbling for the switch of the bedside lamp, she clicked it on and looked at her watch. Nearly two hours had passed since she had left the house on the hill, and Damien had said he would come in an hour's time. Teri switched off the light and lay on her back looking at the stars winking at her through the window, straining her ears, hoping to hear footsteps coming along the passage or the sound of the bedroom door being opened quietly, hoping Damien would come soon and not stay the night with Melina.

At the end of another hour she was aching for him to come and her nerves were stretched to breaking point. Irritated with herself, she got out of bed and went into the bathroom to smoke a cigarette with the door closed so that the smell of it wouldn't go into the bedroom and bring some sharp reprimand from him when he did come. Looking at her face in the mirror above the wash-basin, she laughed jeeringly at herself.

"My God, you look a mess!" she said aloud. "And what's got into you? Why are you so concerned about him, what he thinks about your bad habits—it seems he's got a few himself. So go to bed and stop thinking about him. You're not in love with him. He isn't in love with you, so neither of you should expect too much of each other."

Somehow talking to herself seemed to settle her nerves, because when she lay down again she fell asleep immediately, dropping as if from the top of a mountain down into a deep black abyss to which there was no bottom. Later, much later, she became hazily aware that she was floating up from the bottom of the abyss into wakefulness again and there was warmth behind her. Damien was in bed with her.

"What time is it?" she mumbled sleepily.

"About two o'clock in the morning," he murmured, and slipped a hand over her shoulder. It cupped her breast lightly as he drew her back into the warm curve of his body. "You've been sleeping very heavily."

"I was tired. I'm still tired," she muttered, lifting his hand away and moving towards the edge of the bed. "Goodnight."

He came after her, his arm went round her waist and she felt his lips hot against the cool skin at the back of her neck. She lay rigidly, not at all sleepy any more, hearing the deep thud of Damien's heart and the swift panic-beat of her own. She could feel the passion pulsing through him, feel its heat rising within herself.

"Please go away," she said with a gasping sound as if she were suffocating. "I don't want you."

Tensely she waited, wondering what she would do if he chose to force himself on her. Slowly he withdrew his arm from her waist and she felt him turn on to his back. There was more silence, then he moved again. Teri felt cold air waft into the bed as he lifted the bedclothes. A spring creaked. The bedclothes were thrown back into place. The door opened and closed quietly. He had gone.

CHAPTER FOUR

NEXT morning Teri woke early. There was no sign of Damien and the door to the smaller bedroom remained uncompromisingly closed. In the bathroom, however, a certain steaminess indicated that it had been used that morning.

When she had washed and had dressed in a simple pleated skirt of pale blue cotton and polyester with a matching shirt-like blouse Teri left the bedroom and went in an exploratory tour of her new home.

Home. Would this group of white cubes clinging to a hillside and connected by a series of stone stairways and separated by small secluded courtyards, paved with intricate mosaics of small coloured tiles and overhung by sweet-smelling jasmine, ever be home to her? Or would she always be a stranger here, as she was now, not sure where to find the room where breakfast might be served or even the kitchen where a meal might be prepared.

The room where she had slept, she discovered, was high up on the hillside and after going down two stairways she came to a courtyard which was larger than the others she had seen and which had an archway through which she could see the sea glinting with sunlight. There she had found Arnie busy potting some geraniums, which he placed in wide pottery bowls patterned with Mycenian designs.

"Morning, Mrs. Nikerios," he greeted her. "Finding your way about?"

"Trying to. Which way do I go for breakfast?"

"You'll find the wife through that doorway there."
He pointed with his trowel and following his direction
Teri stepped through yet another archway into another
square room where ikons and tapestries glowed on
white walls and a small table was set for one.

Hardly had she entered the room than Tina appeared through another doorway carrying a tray.

"Good morning, *kyria*," she said in her thick
voice, and set the tray down on the table. "I hope you
like," she added. "There is Greek coffee, bread, butter and honey. Kyrios Nikerios left this for you."
From the pocket of the long white apron she was
wearing over a black skirt she produced a white envelope and handed it to Teri.

"Oh. He's gone already?" Teri exclaimed. "What
time did he leave?"

"At dawn. He went on the yacht to Piraeus," replied Tina woodenly, and went out of the room.

Alone, Teri sat down at the table. As well as the cup
of thick dark Greek coffee there was an orange,
freshly peeled and divided up into slices, hunks of hot
bread wrapped in a white cloth, a dish of yellow butter
and a pottery jar of creamy-looking honey. Feeling
very hungry, she laid the envelope down and set to.
Within a short time she had eaten everything and had
drunk the sweet coffee. Then she opened the envelope and took out the note which was in it.

"Teri," she read, "It seems that you are still tired,
so I will not waken you to say goodbye this morning. I
hope to find you more rested when I return.

"It occurs to me you might need money. So far I

have not had time to arrange an account for you to draw on. In the meantime feel free to ask Philip Marinatos, my father's secretary, for any funds you require. See you, Friday."

Teri folded the note slowly. The terse sentences, the touch of sarcasm, brought him vividly before her and she looked round half expecting to see him come into the room, that half-mocking, half-sweet crooked smile curving his lips and his black eyes glinting at her sardonically. She knew now that he hadn't been deceived by her excuse of tiredness last night. Opening the note again, she re-read the second sentence and felt a strange excitement quiver along her nerves. Damien hoped to find her more rested on his return. Was he implying that he hoped to find her more co-operative, possibly more responsive to his lovemaking?

She would deal with it when it happened, she thought, with her usual refusal to think ahead, and she stuffed the note into the envelope. Today and all the other days until Friday she was going to make the most of being here. She was going to enjoy herself, go where she liked and do what she wanted. Purposefully she made for the courtyard.

"*Kyria*." Tina spoke behind her.

"Well?" Teri swung round.

"Will you be here for the midday meal?"

"I...er...I'm not sure. I'm going out now, up to the other villa to swim in the pool—Mr. Nikerios senior said I could. After that, I'm not sure. I think it would be best if you didn't prepare anything for me." She paused, finding Tina's steady inimical stare irritating. It made her feel as if she was being sized up and censured. "Did you bake the bread for breakfast this morning?" she asked in a rush. There must be some way to break through that cold hostility.

"Yes, I did." There was a slight softening of the severe lines around Tina's mouth.

"It was good. I enjoyed it," said Teri, smiling. "The coffee too. And the honey."

"The honey is from Mount Imitos and is the best in the world," said Tina with quiet pride. "I'm glad you liked it. Is there anything I can do for you today? Have you any clothes to be washed?"

"Only a few pieces of underwear. But I can do those myself if you'll show me where to do the washing."

"It is best if I do it for you, *kyria*. That is why I am here—to look after the house, prepare the meals and do the washing. I do it for Kyrios Nikerios when he stays here. Now that you are his wife I do it for you."

"Yes, but...." Teri began, and broke off to chew at her lower lip. Then she laughed. "The truth of it is, Tina, I'm not used to having everything done for me. I'm used to looking after myself, doing my own washing, cleaning my own place, cooking my own meals. I like to go and come as I please too."

Tina's glance was darkly troubled as she picked up her loaded tray.

"I can see that you are independent, *kyria*," she said quietly. "But you would do well to curb your natural liveliness and friendliness while you stay here alone on the island. There are some who might comment on it and cause trouble for you. Leave the clothes you want washed in the wicker basket in the corner of the bedroom. I'll collect them when I go to make the bed and dust the furniture."

Putting the woman's remarks out of her mind and telling herself that it was because Tina was over-possessive where Damien was concerned that she worried about what people might say about his new wife, Teri went back to her room, collected her swimsuit and a towel and then set off along the path through the pines to the other villa.

Seen from the shade of the cool and pungent pines the walls of Stephanos Nikerios's island home glowed like pale amber in the sunlight and its roofs, all at different levels because the house was terraced like the smaller one, were rose-red. The delicately carved pillars of its archways gave it an insubstantial ethereal quality, and as she approached it Teri almost expected it to vanish before her eyes.

She was directed by another dark, squat Greek housekeeper to a secluded courtyard where jasmine tumbled over white walls, its yellow flowers glinting like stars against green glossy leaves and geranium petals freckled the blue and white mosaic tiles surrounding the swimming pool. Paul was already there, lying on the cushions of a wicker lounger. He was dressed only in the briefest of swimming shorts and taut muscles rippled beneath his bronze skin as he swung off the lounger and came towards her.

He greeted her as he had left her the previous night, lifting her right hand in his and raising it to his lips.

"I'll never get used to it," said Teri, laughing a little selfconsciously and pulling her hand from his. "I'm just not the type of woman who can take having her hand kissed by a strange man gracefully. I suspect it's because I believe too much in equality and don't see myself as some sort of goddess set on a pedestal to be worshipped."

"You look even better by daylight," he murmured, his indigo blue eyes seeming to feast on her hair and her face. "As pure and white as untouched snow. Are you untouched, Teri?" he asked provocatively. "In spite of the fact that you are now a married woman are you still a virgin?"

"*That* is none of your business," she retorted coolly. "Is there anywhere I can change?" she asked, looking around.

"He was late, wasn't he?" he went on. By daylight he also looked different, his lean narrow face reminding her of pictures she had seen in books of Greek mythology, not of Adonis but of a satyr, mischievous and lustful.

"Who was late?" she countered.

"Damien. Last night. He didn't leave this villa until after midnight, stayed here much longer than the hour he told you he would be."

"I haven't the slightest idea," she replied airily. "I was asleep when he returned."

"*Wow!*" Paul remarked, suddenly going all American. "What a way to spend your wedding night!"

"How would you like your ears boxed?" said Teri with pretended sweetness, her eyes beginning to sparkle dangerously. "Any more remarks like that and you can swim by yourself!"

"Okay, okay," he said, grinning at her as he backed away holding up his hands as if to fend off any blows she might deliver. "I won't say another word. You can change in that room over there, through that sliding glass door."

By the time she came out of the room dressed in her clinging black one-piece swimsuit Paul was already swimming about in the limpid blue water. Teri tested the water with a toe and finding it surprisingly tepid dived in from where she stood.

For the next half hour they swam and played happily in the pool, chasing each other and competing in diving exhibitions, but at last, feeling she had had enough exercise, Teri made for the steps, cleaving swiftly through the water. A hand caught at one of her feet and, spluttering, she sank. When she surfaced Paul was with her, hands at her waist, his intention expressed clearly in the sensuous narrowing of his eyes.

She let him kiss her and as soon as it was over slipped from his grasp and struck out for the steps again. He was close behind her when she pulled herself up the steps and she felt his fingers at her ankle again.

"Don't you dare!" she gasped, and kicked backwards, pushing her foot hard against his shoulder. Then she hurried up the steps and bumped into someone who was standing close to them watching.

"Oh, excuse me," she said breathlessly, turning and flinging her wet hair behind her shoulders, and she looked right into the sad fathomless tawny-brown eyes of Melina. At once she stiffened, wondering how long Melina had been standing watching herself and Paul playing in the pool, and wariness made her skin prickle all over.

Melina was beautiful in her Middle-Eastern way, she thought. As tall as herself, she had a full-breasted shapely figure, seen to advantage in the simple silky dress she was wearing. Her facial features were finely carved, the nose having a slight downward curve, and there were interesting hollows in her long cheeks. About the same age as Damien, she would have much in common with him; the same heritage and language and a shared concern about the health of Stephanos. It was only natural that they should be friends and want to talk when they met, quietly and secretively. But had it been necessary for them to talk until after midnight?

Teri became aware that the woman was speaking to her and that she couldn't understand a word.

"What's she saying?" she cried, turning to Paul who was now out of the pool and towelling his hair. "Oh, please tell me what she's saying!"

"She's asking you to stay and have lunch with us, that's all. My grandfather has sent her to invite you to stay. What shall I tell her? Will you stay? And then afterwards we can walk over to the site of the excavated palace."

"Yes, please tell her I'd like to stay."

Paul translated quickly. Melina nodded, said something sharply to him and walked away to the house, managing somehow to express her disapproval by the way she walked.

"Now what?" asked Teri with a sigh, picking up her own towel and beginning to pat herself dry. "It sounded to me as if she was telling you off about something."

"She was—for kissing you." He flung himself down on his lounger, stretching his legs before him. Hands under his head supporting it, he grinned at her, his eyes dancing with devilment. "She says I should show you more respect."

"So you should, since I'm your half-aunt by marriage." Teri retorted mockingly. "But surely she must have realised it was only in fun."

"The way Melina looks at things a man doesn't kiss a woman in fun and a woman doesn't kiss him back, like you did, in fun, either. Now she probably has you sized up as one of those liberated Northern women who sleeps around while her husband is away."

"Sleeping around is something she would never do, of course," said Teri scathingly, picking up her handbag and taking out her cigarettes.

"Only with the man she loves," Paul replied dryly. "And he happens to be Damien."

Disturbed by what he was saying, Teri lit a cigarette, slipped on her sun-glasses and stretched out on the other lounger.

"How marvellous to be able to sunbathe at this time of the year," she said lightly, determined to change the subject of conversation. "I'd no idea it would be so warm."

From under the shade of his hand his glance roved over her long bare-ivory limbs.

"I should guess that by the end of the week your skin will be the colour of honey and you'll look quite devastating with your silvery hair," he drawled. "Melina is going to have a hard time of it competing with you."

"I wish you'd stop," said Teri between taut lips. "I wish you'd stop going on about her and Damien."

"Jealous already?" he jeered.

"No. Just sick of that sort of conversation. Can't you talk about something else? Do we have a siesta after lunch?"

"No. Siesta doesn't happen until the summer. Late each spring the official hours are anounced by the police. Usually it's between the hours of one-thirty and five p.m. It's considered extremely rude to disturb anyone at home during that time of the day and any undue noisy behaviour at that time is automatically reported to the police," Paul replied in a flat monotone. "Is it time we began the language lessons?" he added, provocative again. "That should keep us both out of mischief for a while, and considering your near-panic just now the sooner you learn some Greek the better."

"All right. Where shall we begin?"

"With the alphabet."

By the time lunch was served in a pleasantly cool,

high-ceilinged room Teri had learned the alphabet and was able to say please and thank you in Greek. Delighted with her own progress; she tried out both words on Melina when the latter either offered or passed food to her, hoping to break through the polite indifference with which the woman treated her. But her success with Tina was not to be repeated; Melina did not soften or smile. Throughout the meal she maintained a straight face and a stony silence, not even bothering to respond to Stephanos's rather risqué jokes.

The meal being the main one of the day consisted of several courses. First there was onion soup with grated cheese. That was followed by a *souvlaka* of sweet juicy chunks of lamb skewered together with mushrooms, spiced with lemons and herbs. The meat was served with fried potatoes and a tomato salad. When she had eaten her share Teri felt full and had difficulty in doing justice to the *halvas*, a sort of loaf made with nuts and honey, but she enjoyed the misted blue grapes which followed with the usual Greek coffee.

"And where is Paul going to take you this afternoon?" Stephanos boomed at Teri. "We can't have you being bored, you know, while Damien is away. We have to keep you busy so that you don't pine for him."

"We're going to walk over to the palace which was excavated by Carl Sweiss," said Teri.

"Ever meet him?" asked Stephanos.

"No, never."

"An interesting man, Carl," he went on. "Clever too, but I was glad when he had finished his excavating, went back to Germany and took his wife with him."

"I thought she left him while he was working

here," said Paul. "I'm sure someone told me she eloped with some younger guy."

"Eh? What's that you say?" Stephanos gave his grandson a sharp look. "Whom did she elope with?"

"I don't know. I thought you might be able to tell me, Grandfather. After all, you were here at the time."

"Humph! She was nothing but a troublemaker," muttered the old man, shaking his head. "She was the wrong type to be married to a scholar like Carl. She wanted attention all the time and when she couldn't get it flaunted herself at the other men. Melina, I feel tired. I think I'd like to go and have a rest. My stomach is bothering me, too." He turned and smiled at Teri suddenly and for a moment in the warmth of that smile she saw a resemblance to Damien and felt a new ache gnaw inside her. For several seconds she longed for Damien to be there with them. Then the desire passed as quickly as it had come.

The way to the palace wound upwards dusty and rough, twisting between reddish brown rocks and through groves of olives and groups of bent, wind-twisted pines. It led them on to a natural plateau several feet above sea level from which they could see the red roofs of the fishing village shimmering in the sunlight and beyond them the sea stretching blue and silver, blindingly bright.

The restored palace was disappointingly small and consisted of a few pillars of apricot-coloured stone standing about what had once been a mosaic-covered courtyard and a few crumbling walls. There was no sound, no breath of wind, nothing to disturb the warm tranquillity of the afternoon.

"I wonder who lived here," said Teri. "In his book Carl Sweiss suggested it was a summer palace, one to which a king from the mainland came when the weather became unbearably hot."

"Like the kings of today, the millionaires and big-shot industrialists who have their hideaways among the islands, you mean. Like Grandfather and Damien have their villas here. Could be, I suppose." Paul's face crinkled with mocking amusement. "Just imagine old Agamemnon sneaking away from Myceae to this place. You know, there must have been times when he was glad to get away from that old hag Clytemnestra."

"I've always believed he deserved what happened to him for sacrificing his own daughter," retorted Teri, looking round the silent, sunlit place. "Have you been to Mycenae? Is it like this?"

"Very similar, only on a larger scale." Paul glanced up at the tops of the pillars which seemed to be moving against the high blue sky. "The pillars are the same period. But there's no tomb here to visit."

"And no ghosts," said Teri.

"Except the ghosts of Carl and Helga Sweiss," he replied as they strolled from the courtyard and down another path which twisted among stunted trees along the edge of a cliff, from which there was a sheer drop into the sea. "I wonder what really happened here that summer they were excavating? Every time I try to find out members of the family who know about it, my mother, her sister, and Grandfather get very hush-hush. It's one of those secrets which must not be divulged to the young. You know the sort of thing I'm talking about?"

"I think so. They don't want you to know that one of them has behaved scandalously in the past. They are, in their own way, protecting your innocence," Teri said.

"A bit late for that," Paul said scoffingly. "I'm a

big boy now and know all about the birds and the bees. What shall we do now? Have you had enough of antiquity for a while? How about tasting the flavour of modern Greece? Like to go down to the fisherman's wharf and have a drink in the *taverna*? That's always a good place to find out what's going on.''

Later, much later, they drove back from the village in one of the horse-drawn carriages. Paul was reluctant to leave Teri, but she managed to persuade him to go back to his grandfather's house by promising to meet him the next morning to swim again. Then with the beat of the *bouzouki* music she had heard at the *taverna* still drumming through her head she made her way to her bedroom.

The next few days followed a similar pattern. Every morning she went up to the big villa to swim in the pool, sunbathe for a while and eat lunch with Stephanos, Melina and Paul. Every afternoon she and Paul explored some part of the island, always ending up at the waterfront in the village to talk with the fishermen and be entertained by *bouzouki* music and dancing.

By the time Thursday night came Teri felt she had had enough of life on the island and was suffering from acute boredom. The trouble was she wasn't used to doing nothing. Sleepless and restless, she lay in bed watching the stars swing past the window and wished she was back in London, working at Hayton's. She was missing the people she knew, her mother, her working colleagues, her friends. In spite of Paul's friendliness and Stephanos's almost smothering kindness and generosity she still felt like a stranger.

It would be better when Damien came back, she assured herself. Once he came he would take her to all those other places she wanted to see in Greece that she had read about for years. It would be better when he was with her, he would know how to assuage this awful aching restlessness she was suffering from, and tomorrow he would come. He had said he would.

Next morning she didn't go swimming as usual with Paul but stayed in her room and wrote letters to her mother, her brother and her friend Shirley. Only after lunch did she walk up the path to the other villa.

"Why didn't you come to swim this morning?" Paul asked sulkily.

"I had other things to do," she replied coolly.

"Grandfather wants to see you. He's in his study. Philip is just back from Athens and is talking to him, but I don't suppose they'll mind if you interrupt them."

Teri found her way to Stephanos's cool book-lined study. As usual he was pleased to see her, holding out his arms to her affectionately so that she went to him and kissed him on the cheek, but when he told her that there was a message from Damien saying he would not be returning from New York until Monday she could have cried with disappointment.

"Why?" she asked, her voice shaking a little in spite of herself. "Why is he delayed?"

"He couldn't get through the business in time to catch the plane which would have brought him back last night," Stephanos explained patiently, and squeezed her hand gently. "Don't mind too much, my dear. He'll be here soon. Sometimes business has to come first. You're disappointed because you haven't long been married. Once you have been together for a while and you have a family to think about, something to occupy you, you won't miss him so much."

"But I'm not...." Teri broke off, biting her lip. She had been about to blurt out that she wasn't going to have a family and then had realised she would be betraying herself. She looked up and found the sharp black eyes watching her closely.

"A boy, that's what I'd like," Stephanos whispered. "A son of my son. You know where I come from, Teri?"

"No." She shook her head.

"I come from Mani in the Peloponneses. The Maniotes are poor people, but magnanimous and dignified, despite the poverty in which they live, and they claim descent from the warlike Spartans. Even now they welcome male children by gunfire salutes and boys are referred to as 'guns'. I'm hoping you and Damien are going to have a little 'gun' later this year. Perhaps he'll be born on my birthday. That's the twenty-sixth of December, Saint Stephen's Day. I hope you'll call him Stephanos after me and that I'll hold him in my arms before I die."

Teri stared at him, transfixed by the glitter in his eyes, held stationary by his hand on her arm, her whole being revolting against what he was suggesting.

"That's why I've been on to Damien to get married," Stephanos went on in the same hoarse whisper. "He's been the playboy long enough." His dark glance slid over her, resting meaningfully on her flat stomach and narrow hips. "But I'm not sure about you." His eyes flicked upwards to her face. "You're pretty, but you're not very wide where it matters. Too highly bred, perhaps. Damien could have made a mistake in choosing you, in more ways than one. You don't seem to have much stamina or staying power. Like that son of my daughter, young Paul, you belong to this generation, what do they call it? The *Now* generation? Can't get things fast enough and then when you've got 'em you don't want 'em. No, unless you change, you're not good enough for my son Damien."

"That isn't true!" Teri flashed, pulling her hand free of his. "I have got stamina and staying power. I...I...I've suffered a lot in the past two years, but I've survived."

The thick lips curved into a mocking grin and he slapped his thigh suddenly with one hand.

"That's better," he chortled. "That's what I like to see—some spirit. So how are you going to put in time until Monday? Getting tired of this place, aren't you?"

"A little." Like Damien, he noticed too much, was far too observant for his own good. "I'm used to working, doing things for myself, going where I want when I want."

"And where would you like to go?"

"To...to Athens...to look at the museums, the Acropolis."

"All right...so go there, tomorrow. Young Paul knows how. You can go and see my house where you'll live when Damien comes back. You can stay there in his rooms. As long as you're around when he comes back Monday there's no reason why you shouldn't go where you want when you want while he's away. That suit you?"

"Yes...it would...thank you." Teri found she was stuttering and looked at him again to find the dark eyes twinkling at her. Devious old man that he was, he had guessed at her restlessness and was offering a remedy. He understood how she felt and wanted to help. "You're very kind," she added belatedly, feeling all her earlier revulsion to him fade away in the face of this new example of his generosity.

"I'm doing it for Damien," he whispered. "I'm doing it for him. I don't want you leaving him like his mother left me, because she was bored and lonely.

Now go on, get out of here and let me have my afternoon snooze. I haven't had a bit of peace all day with all the comings and goings."

Teri found Paul in his usual place, lying on a lounger by the pool sipping a long, ice-clinking drink through a straw, his face marred by an expression of extreme boredom.

"Damien isn't coming back till Monday," she said as she settled herself on another lounger, "so I think I'll go to Athens and stay there for a couple of days. Your grandfather says you can tell me how to get there."

"Sure I can," he said, sitting up and giving her a bright-eyed look, all the boredom gone from his face. "Mind if I come with you? There's a couple of guys I was with at college staying there. They arrived yesterday. I was thinking of going over anyway tomorrow. We can travel together. Angelos Skopelos, the big fisherman who was dancing last night at the *taverna*, will take us to Aegina and from there we can get the hydrofoil. We can be in the capital in a couple of hours after leaving here. Where were you thinking of staying?"

"In Damien's suite in the Nikerios villa."

"Good. I guess I can put up there too." Paul sipped the rest of his drink down noisily and then rolled off the lounger. "Come on," he said. "Let's go and make the arrangements with Angelos now."

Next morning the blue and white caique belonging to Angelos Skopolos chugged fussily across the smooth blue water of the Skios harbour, its single mast swaying slightly from side to side, its engine backfiring noisily and sending out a cloud of smelly black smoke. Teri had hoped the portly, moustachioed Angelos would have put up his sail and that they would have drifted silently and romantically down-wind to the island of Aegina. But as Paul pointed out, there was hardly any wind and he didn't want to waste time flopping about on the sea for the next few hours. He wanted to get to Athens.

Three quarters of an hour later the other island, lush green and mountainous, appeared as if by magic through the pearly sunlit mist, the pale cubes of its houses looking like a child's square building blocks piled one on top of the other, climbing the hillside behind the harbour. The caique swept into the harbour, curved around some moored boats and came to a stop at the wharf. Within fifteen minutes Teri and Paul, with their small amount of luggage, were aboard the hydrofoil, with a crowd of islanders who were going to the capital to shop, and were skimming at high speed over the now brilliantly blue water. Thirty-five minutes later they were ashore at Piraeus and jumping into a taxi were on their way to the Nikerios villa in the outskirts of Athens.

Months afterwards, looking back to that day she spent with Paul in Athens, it seemed to Teri it was the last day of her youth, the last day she felt irresponsible, the last day she spent without a thought for anyone else, for past or for future; the last day before she fell in love for the second time in her life.

The Nikerios villa was situated in the modern part of Athens near Mount Likavitos and was one of a number of dazzlingly white houses half hidden by white walls and dark cypress trees which commanded a magnificent view across the city to the Acropolis.

Inside the house was so big that Teri felt overawed and dwarfed as she stood in the entrance hall with its intricate mosaic floor and soaring white pillars while Paul explained who she was to the housekeeper.

But the woman was welcoming, far more so than
Tina had been at first, and took her up a wide stairway
which had a beautiful banister of veined marble and
along a wide corridor to the suite of rooms which be-
longed to Damien.

"Will you be staying long, *kyria*?" the housekeeper
asked in careful English.

"Tonight and perhaps tomorrow night. I...I'm not
sure yet. It depends on when Dam...my husband returns," said Teri. "I'll let you know," she added more
assertively, trying to remember that as Damien's wife
she was mistress in this house and could command
any service she wanted.

She was glad to find that the suite was furnished in a
comfortable homely style and had a feeling of being
lived in. There were two bedrooms, as there were at the
villa on Skios; a large one, furnished with a wide king-
sized bed covered in blue and white damask, and a
smaller one also containing a double bed which was
covered in a soft apricot colour, a room that was much
softer, less uncompromisingly masculine than the big-
ger one. Between the two rooms there was a bathroom
and both bedrooms opened into a small passageway
which led to a sitting room which had a balcony from
which she had her first breathtaking view of the Acropolis soaring above the forest of concrete high-rise
buildings of the modern Athens.

She had just finished unpacking the few clothes she
had brought and had hung them in the closet in the
apricot and cream room when there was a knock on
the outer door of the sitting room. Guessing it was
Paul, she went through to open the door.

"All settled in?" he queried. "Where would you
like to go first?"

"The Acropolis, of course."

"Have I your permission to borrow Damien's car to drive you about the city? It's down in the garage doing nothing, along with Grandfather's limousine."

"My permission?" queried Teri. "Why my permission?"

"You're his wife, so I guess what's his is yours and what's yours is his," Paul retorted cheekily. "Of course we could use public transport, but it would mean waiting about."

"Do you think he would mind if we used it?" she asked cautiously.

"We'll face that one when we come to it, shall we?" with something of her own impetuous attitude.

"All right, we'll borrow it. I suppose someone has the keys."

"You suppose right. Andros, Grandfather's chauffeur, has them. He has all the fun around here—gets to drive all the cars one at a time, when no one is using them, just to keep them in running order."

There was a certain amount of exhilaration to be gained from whisking through the Saturday morning traffic in the low-slung sports car, narrowly avoiding other cars which were darting along the narrow streets as they plunged down towards the main throughfare which would take them to Syntagma Square.

"We'll come back here for lunch, at one of those cafés," Paul shouted to her above the din of traffic. With his curls lifting in the breeze and a faint smile curving his mouth he was obviously in his element driving the fast car. "We're meeting Chuck and Lily there. I phoned them from the house." He wrenched the steering wheel round and they roared along another narrow street, past neatly whitewashed old houses and the entrances to twisting narrow alleyways. "This is the Plaka," Paul explained. "It used to be all there was of

Athens at one time. It's at its best at night, when the *tevernas* open. We'll come back here this evening for supper. There'll be music and dancing then.''

They parked the car and joined a group of tourists, mostly elderly Germans and Americans, who were having their holidays in the spring before the mad rush of tourists came for the summer, to walk up the ramp to Athena's shrine, pausing at a battlement on the right from where, the guide told them, King Aegeus saw the black sails on the sea which Theseus his son had forgotten to change on his return from Crete. Believing his son to have been killed by the Minotaur, Aegeus then plunged to his death in an excess of grief.

"Come on," Paul urged at Teri's shoulder. "Let's go on by ourselves. I can tell you all there is to know. And anyway, once you're living here permanently you can come every day if you want."

Teri didn't need persuading. She went with him to linger in awed silence to stare at the soaring columns of Pendelic marble which formed the Parthenon. It was true the stone was badly eroded by the pollution from modern industry, but the place still held mystery and magic.

"You should come at sunset," said Paul as they wandered on to the Temple of the Wingless Victory. "Or later in the season to one of the Son et Lumière presentations."

Teri wished Damien was with her instead of Paul. The thought flitted through her mind and was gone, leaving her feeling bewildered. Why did she think she could enjoy being in this place any more if he were with her? She didn't have to have anyone with her to enjoy it and get the most out of it; she had learned that the hard way after David had died. No one person was going to mean more to her than any other for the rest of her life. No one person was going to mean more to her than herself. She had vowed that the day she should have been married to David. It hurt too much to love someone more than yourself. It hurt when they went away or died.

"Let's go back to that square...what did you call it? Syntagma?" she said, turning impulsively to Paul. "Let's go and meet your friends."

He looked surprised.

"But we haven't looked at everything here yet," he said. "We haven't been to the museum, or to the Theatre of Dionysus."

"I've seen enough." said Teri imperiously. "Come on."

He went with her without further argument, and it wasn't long before they were sitting in one of the busy *kafenions* in the square sitting at a table at the back of the room. All along one of the walls big glass doors gave out on the pavement and as they drank their soft drink they were able to watch all Athens, or so it seemed, go by. Fashionably dressed women and peasant women in black skirts and black headscarfs, businessmen impeccably dressed and working men in rough clothes. Everyone was talking both inside the café and outside, shouting, laughing, gesticulating.

Teri loved it. In the noise and bustle of people she could forget herself and her problems. Paul's friends arrived, the young man long-haired and bearded, dressed in the inevitable jeans, T-shirt and denim jacket, the girl with smooth long-flowing honey-coloured hair and a wide beautiful smile, both of them excited by this their first visit to Greece.

After lunch somehow they all crammed into the sports car and roared off out of the city along the coastal road to Cape Sounion, which snakes through the beach resorts of that area, leaving them behind to dip down beside lovely little coves, which had so far escaped commercial development. Mountains of white salt glittered above the salt pans of Anavisis and then they were at Sounion at last where, in spite of the ugly tourist additions, the pillars of the Temple of Poseidon were still pure white and still, as impressive against the deep blue of the sky as they had been when Byron had seen them and had set a bad example by carving his name on them.

They managed to linger at Sounion to see the sun set on one side of the temple and the moon rise on the other and then drove back to Athens, arriving in the Plaka just as the *tavernas* opened at nine-thirty. Paul took them to his favourite. It had a dirt floor and rows of huge wine barrels were part of the decoration. The food, though simple, was excellent and they ate *moussaka*, drank *retsina*, and when the dancing began joined in.

At midnight, since it was Easter Eve, they spilled with everyone else into the streets, to surge along in the direction of Mount Lycabettus to see the craggy hillside light up with thousands of candles carried by people returning from services at the Church of St. George while cannons boomed out the news of the Resurrection of Christ.

It was after one in the morning when Teri and Paul returned to the Nikerios villa. Inside the entrance hall was dimly lit and they went quietly up the stairs. At the doorway to the suite of rooms which were reserved for Damien, Teri turned to say goodnight. At once Paul seized hold of her and kissed her boisterously and inexpertly.

"Let me come in with you and stay the rest of the

night with you," he said, not bothering to lower his voice.

"Don't be silly!" she retorted, pushing him away, and turning the doorknob eased the door open slowly.

"It isn't silly," he objected, moving after her. "I've fallen in love with you and I want you. We've had fun together today and...."

"Haven't you forgotten something?" she interrupted coolly. "I happen to be married to a relative of yours...."

"A marriage of convenience, a business arrangement—you told me that yourself, so there's nothing to stop you from having relationships with other men," argued Paul. "And what do you think Damien has been doing while he's been in New York? Surely you don't believe he's been saving it all for you? He probably has a mistress there...."

"Goodnight."

Teri spoke emphatically as she slid through the opening of the door and before he could follow her into the room she closed the door in his face. Groping, she found a key and she turned it quickly in the lock. Then she leaned against the door, fully expecting Paul to start banging on it and to shout through it to her, knowing he had had enough to drink to make him reckless of what the servants in the house might think of such behaviour.

He didn't bang, but he did rattle the door knob and call to her.

"Teri, don't be so mean!"

"I'm not being mean. I'm sleepy and I'd like to have a good night's rest if we're going to set out for Delphi early tomorrow. You should go to sleep too, since you're going to do all the driving. I'll see you at breakfast," she replied. "Goodnight."

"Oh, okay." Paul sounded sulky. "I suppose you're right."

"I know I am."

"Goodnight, then," he growled.

Teri stayed where she was with her back to the room, leaning against the door, straining her ears for the sound of footsteps going away. She didn't hear anything except the beating of her own heart and eventually she decided that Paul had gone.

Letting out a sigh, she turned away from the door into the room and felt the chill of sheer fright freeze her blood. Silhouetted against the glow of city lights in the sky beyond the wide window were the head and shoulders of a man. In breathless silence she stared wondering whether it was her imagination playing tricks on her or the combination of light and shadow in the room. Then the silhouette moved, became one with the shadows and she heard the stealthy pad of feet coming across the carpet towards her.

Teri stood still, wanting to speak and yet unable to force the words from her dry throat. There was a click and a table lamp came on, its yellow light slanting outwards and downwards, illuminating the other person from the waist downwards, showing that he was wearing dark pyjama pants and a three quarter-length black velour dressing robe. Above the waist he was still shadowy, but she was able to recognise him and words burst from her in relief as she stepped towards him.

"Damien, what are you doing here?" she exclaimed. "I was told you wouldn't be back from New York until Monday or Tuesday at the latest."

"I was able to come sooner than expected. I managed to get on a plane to Rome. I flew from there this afternoon and arrived here an hour or so ago. It was too late for me to set out for Skios, so I decided to spend the night here. I'd no idea you were here. I must have been asleep for about half an hour when I heard you and Paul talking at the door."

In the slanting light she could see now that his hair was ruffled, he needed a shave and his eyelids were heavy.

"Didn't the housekeeper tell you I was here?" she asked.

"No. Perhaps she assumed I knew that you were." His mouth took on its sardonic curve. "And now it's my turn," he added softly, coming over to her. "What are you doing here?"

"It was your father's idea that we...Paul and I should come and stay for a day or two."

"I see. And where have you been until this hour?"

"In the Plaka. We've been dancing. And after that we watched the candle procession on Mount Lycabettus. It was a wonderful sight. I've never seen anything like it before."

"I watched it too. There's a good view from the window here," Damien said quietly.

"Oh, I wish I'd known," she began impulsively, and stopped abruptly.

"Wish you'd known what?" he prompted.

"Nothing. It doesn't matter," she said airily. "We had a lovely day. Two of Paul's friends are here, from the States. We went with them to Sounion this afternoon and this morning he and I were at the Acropolis. Tomorrow...." Again she broke off.

"Go on, please," he said. "What are you going to do tomorrow?"

"We talked of...we did plan to drive to Delphi and stay the night there and come back Monday. But now that you're back," she laughed with a touch of nervousness, "we won't be able to go."

"Why not?" asked Damien, shoving his hands into the pockets of his robe and moving away out of the light into the shadow. "Don't let my return stop you from doing anything you've planned to do," he continued, turning in her direction again, but remaining in the shadow so that he could see her but she couldn't see him properly. "Just because you're married to me it doesn't mean that you have to restrict your movements when I'm around. Marriage doesn't mean we have to live in each other's pockets."

"No. I suppose it doesn't," she murmured. "Perhaps I should explain. Today we went about in your sports car and we were going to use it tomorrow. I... I hope you don't mind."

"As long as you don't damage it I have no objection to you using it when I'm not, but I suggest you'd be far more comfortable travelling to Delphi in my father's Cadillac if there are going to be four of you. It's about a hundred and seventy kilometres from Athens. If you like I'll tell the chauffeur you and Paul can borrow it," he drawled.

"Would you? That's very good of you," Teri said warmly, although she was aware suddenly of tension between them. She began to move towards the little hallway along which light was shafting presumably from his bedroom. "I think I overdid the dancing a little tonight," she said. "I'll be glad to get in bed." She half turned towards him as he followed her slowly. "You look tired too. I'm sorry we disturbed you. Was the journey back very tedious?"

"No more than usual," he replied as he switched off the table lamp.

"Then I'll say goodnight," she said, and went purposefully down the hallway to the room where she had left her belongings.

"I'm sleeping in the other room," said Damien, just behind her, his hand closed over hers on the doorknob. "And you are going to sleep with me," he added silkily, bending his head so that the roughness of his cheek brushed hers and she could smell the tang of his skin and hair. "It was wise of you to refuse to sleep with young Paul, but it would be unwise of you to refuse to sleep with me tonight. I've paid for the honour of your company in my bed, and I thought I had made it clear when I asked you to marry me that I aim to get my money's worth."

"Paid?" She spat the word out as she flung back her head to glare at him. In the faint light from the other bedroom his face had that satanic quality she had first noticed and his eyes were so dark, so unreflecting that they seemed like two holes in his head. "What do you mean, you've paid?" she demanded tautly.

"Forgotten our contract already?" he enquired, raising his eyebrows in mock surprise. "Forgotten that I have invested several hundred thousand pounds in a very shaky publishing business? Know what I mean now when I say I have paid to have you share my bed?"

"You...you...bastard!" she raged, trying to twist her hand from under his so she could slap him and failing.

"I wondered when you'd get down to my level with your language," he mocked, and curved his other hand about her throat so that she couldn't move her head. Bending forward, he brushed his lips tantalisingly across hers. "Don't let's fight, Teri," he whispered. "Let's make love instead."

"No, I...."

"You're too tired," he remarked dryly. "Is that

what you were going to say?'' His fingers pressed insinuatingly against her gullet, almost cutting off her breath, then slid downwards to fondle the hollow at the base of her throat. ''I let that excuse pass the other night because I knew you had had a difficult day. But it won't pass tonight. Come to bed with me. You may think you don't want to, but once we're lying together with our arms around each other as we did that night in London, you'll want to, you'll be pleading with me to do it.''

Teri was shaking all over with the effort to resist the seductive touch of his fingers.

''Please give me a few minutes...to change into a nightgown,'' she said, trying to sound cool and determined.

''And to keep me waiting? Or perhaps to lock the doors against me?'' he jeered. ''No way.'' His fingers squeezed hers on the knob to turn it. As the door opened he pushed her before him into the unlit room. The door closed behind him with a click. ''One bed is as good as another to sleep on, I guess,'' he said with a hint of laughter in his voice, and then his arms curved strongly about her and she was hauled against him.

''This is the first time in my life I have had a wife to come home to after my travels,'' he whispered, stroking her hair tenderly away from her ears. ''Make me welcome, Teri.''

Although his kiss was fiery sweet and his appeal went straight to her generous vulnerable heart she still resisted, afraid of the consequences if she gave in and let her own passion rise up to meet his.

''Have you missed me?'' he asked, hardly lifting his mouth from hers to speak.

''Not at all,'' she lied coolly, and tried to push free of him.

"You will next time I go away," he retorted, and she felt the hot taste of his breath on her lips. "I'm going to make damn sure of that now."

It burst out then, the hot Greek fire, and scorched her. His fingers found and pinched the point of one of her breasts so that she gasped and swayed, her mouth lifting blindly in the direction of his even while she continued to deny him.

"No, Damien, not yet—" she began, but he was past hearing, and as the savagery of his next kiss tore at the fullness of her lips her own desire overwhelmed her and with a smothered cry of pleasure she moulded herself against the firmness of his hard body, her hands sliding within the lapels of his robe to fondle his bare, hair-crisped chest. This was what she had been aching for last night, this closeness, this freedom to touch and caress, this sweet sensuousness melting the hard old core of resistance, until every tender nerve ending in the secret places of her body was inflamed and clamouring for his touch.

Even then she tried to make a last-minute withdrawal, tried to obey the small voice of caution which kept reminding her she was in danger and that a situation like this was what she had intended to avoid. But Damien would not let her go. His own passion, now far beyond his control, gave him a Herculean strength which overcame her completely, stripping her of her clothing, whirling her across the room in a sort of wild dance to the bed across which they both fell in pagan abandon, unashamedly naked in the light-dappled darkness, sighing and groaning, limbs moving and entwining in the sweet agony of physical desire.

More than once they reached the peaks of ecstasy that night, and the pale fingers of pearly dawn light were silvering the walls of the room before they both fell asleep suddenly like two children who have played too long and too strenuously. Silver had changed to gold when Teri opened her eyes again, disturbed by knocking on the door and a voice shouting her name, but she was too sunk in a delicious lethargy, too comfortable to move or to answer.

"It's Paul," Damien murmured, his lips moving against the swell of her breast, the stiff stubble of his beard rasping her soft skin. "Do you still want to go to Delphi with him today?"

"No. I want to stay with you," she whispered, lazily running fingers through the tangle of his black hair.

"How very wise of you, Mrs. Nikerios," he mocked softly, raising his head to look at her through slanting black lashes, his expression changing, eyes glowing hot with desire as he saw her gilded by sunlight. He muttered something in Greek and his mouth closed over hers and the flames of passion were once again leaping up to consume them when the shouting and banging began again.

"I'll deal with him," Damien muttered, and slid off the bed. Teri was drifting off into a doze when he came back, reaching for her, gathering her against him closely, his hands caressing the softly rounded curves of her body.

"What did you say to him?" she asked.

"I told him you couldn't come because you were going on your honeymoon with me," he told her.

"Honeymoon?" she exclaimed, sitting up suddenly, half turning to look down at him, unaware of the seduction of her pose, pink-tipped breasts slightly tilted, smooth legs curved under her, one arm supporting her, her hair seeming to blaze with white fire in the sunlight, her sun-kissed skin shining like gold.

Flat on his back, his hands under his head, Damien lay looking at her, his glance moving over her possessively.

"That's right," he replied. "Most couples start their marriage with a honeymoon."

"Yes, but only if they're in love with each other," she argued.

"So? Aren't we in love?" he countered.

Her eyes wavered away from his, their glance drifting down over his wide chest, dark with rough hairs, on the the flat smooth-skinned stomach, the sinewy thighs and legs also dark with hairs, and remembering how his body, pulsing with passion, had entwined with hers during the night, she felt desire begin to uncoil again within her.

"No, I don't think we are. We don't know one another well enough to be in love," she muttered, averting her eyes from his dark male beauty, her hands clenching on her knees as she fought the longing to throw herself down upon him.

"You have to know a person before you can love him, is that what you're saying?" he queried.

"Yes."

"For me it is different," he said softly, taking a hand from behind his head and stroking the curve of her thigh suggestively. "For me, all it takes is one look, and I am in love."

"But that isn't love," she objected, swinging round to look at him, her breath catching in her throat as fingers found potent nerves and as his her eyes encountered the blatant desire expressed in his.

"What is it, then?" he whispered.

"It...it's just physical desire," she sighed, giving into the feeling of voluptuousness which was sweeping through her, softening her limbs so that she swayed forward until her breasts brushed against his chest and her parted lips hovered above his.

"And the beginning of loving," he said, putting his arms around her and holding her down against him so that her head whirled under an onslaught of new sensations. "It's good, hmm? This touching and feeling each other?" he whispered. "We make love together well?"

"It's good," she gasped, and pressed her mouth against his.

CHAPTER FIVE

Two months later Teri sat beside the swimming pool at Stephanos's villa on the island of Skios reading a letter. It was from her brother Dick, and the light flippant way in which he wrote made her mouth curve in a smile of affection.

He had managed to get through the last year at school without dishonouring the name of Hayton and hoped to do fairly well in his 'A' level exams. He hoped to go and work at Hayton's after leaving school. He had excelled himself at sports and hoped Teri would come to Brookhill for the annual sports day to see him perform in the running races. He expected to win both the mile and the fifteen thousand metres. Hadn't he read somewhere that Damien Nikerios had once been a runner and had once taken part in the Olympic marathon as well as having represented Greece in various athletic meetings when he had been younger?

Teri lowered the letter and stared frowningly at the glinting water of the pool. Damien a runner? He had never said anything to her about taking part in the Olympic Games. Neither had anyone else. But she remembered suddenly his reply to the comments she had made about him being a fast runner, the morning after their first meeting. "*I'm not as fast as I was*," he had said casually.

Leaning back, she closed her eyes. The June sun was hot and soon she would have to take cover in the house, but meanwhile she had a few moments to herself for sun-worship. The air was heady with the scent of flowers which were blooming profusely in the courtyard gardens and beyond the walls the pines sighed softly in the sea breeze.

Damien an athlete. Yes, knowing now so intimately the muscular perfection of his physique, knowing how he loved to swim and dive, having seen him dance *bouzouki* in island *tavernas* when they were on their honeymoon, keeping up with and even often surpassing local fishermen renowned for their stamina, it was easy to believe.

But he had never told her. In fact he had told her very little about himself; he was not a great talker, so that when they had returned from the two-week cruise they had taken among the Aegean islands on the Nikerios motor yacht, Teri had known no more about him than when they had left.

Yet it had been a time out of mind, their so-called honeymoon, and looking back now it seemed to her that those two weeks had been among the happiest of her life and memories of it often flicked before her mind's eye like photographic slides. It had been a time she would remember always, no matter what happened in the future.

Leaving Piraeus, they had made their way leisurely among the islands. One of her favourites had been Delos with its remnants of past glory, the marble fragments of ancient temples, exquisite mosaics, a place of silent ruins adorned by a row of marble lions, glowing in the rosy light of the setting sun. Naxos too had attracted her, green terraces ridging steep hillsides, the snow-white cubes, cupolas and archways of its houses stark against the brilliant blue of the sky.

Lindos, on the island of Rhodes, had been set in a

turquoise sea, spreading below the ochre-coloured ramparts of an old fortress which had guarded the ruins of a columned temple and the water had been so deep that the yacht had anchored quite close to the shore. Teri and Damien had gone ashore to ride donkeys up the hill to the ancient acropolis and to look down from dizzying heights to the few boats anchored off the shore.

Of the city of Rhodes itself all she remembered was the entrance to Mandraki harbour with the twin towers on either side, topped by the sculptures of deer, the lights of the shopping arcades crowding about the harbour winking through the dusk beneath the brooding silhouette of the Crusaders' castle and the narrow streets of the old town cluttered with *tavernas* and gift shops.

But it was the smaller islands, the less commercialised and less inhabited ones she had enjoyed the most, and there were memories of friendly island people, luscious seafood, tasty *souvlaki*; of the heady resinated wine, the gift of the god Dionysus to the Greeks; and above all memories of making love with Damien, in sheer pagan abandonment, anywhere and everywhere, but always resenting after the act the power he had over her, a power he used whenever he could to enslave her.

Theirs was a purely physical relationship, she was beginning to accept that now, and every time she found herself wishing it could be more she squashed the wish before it could develop into something like regret, swatting it as she might swat an irritating fly. Damien had bought her. She was his possession and he treated her as such. It was a humiliating and shameful position for her to be in, she admitted, but it would pass, it would soon come to an end... when she left him.

Meanwhile she could play the game he wanted to play as well as he could. A woman could make love and then go on her way regardless, just like a man could, without letting her emotions become involved.

When they had returned to Athens, much to her surprise, he hadn't taken her to the Nikerios villa but to another smaller house, a modernised version of the traditional Greek house with thick white walls, archways and outdoor staircases, and flower-filled courtyards, screened from the roadway which wound up Mount Lykavitos, by cultivated cypresses and pines. She had been delighted with everything about it, the size, the up-to-date arrangement of the rooms, the luxuriousness of the furnishings, and she had said so.

"It is yours," Damien had said simply.

"Yours too," she had replied.

"No, just yours."

"But...." She had been puzzled.

"I am giving it to you as a belated wedding present. The house is in your name and if you ever want to sell it you will receive the proceeds," he had replied coolly.

"But surely you will live here too, when we're in Athens?" Teri had exclaimed.

"Sometimes, yes, when I want to be with you." He had come over to her, to look at her with half closed eyes in which the hot fire of his desire glittered. "Like now," he had whispered, and even as his lips had touched hers his hand had been busy sliding undone the zip at the back of the dress she had been wearing.

Sometimes he had been there, with her. That was how it had been. He had not shared the house with her as a husband should have done and so had made it very clear how he regarded their relationship. It was a convenience, and she was no more after all than a mistress.

Teri shifted restlessly on the lounger, opening her eyes and picking up Dick's letter which had fallen from her hand. Glancing through it, she noted the date of the Brookhill Sports Day. It would take place two weeks from now and she would be there. Going to see Dick run would be her excuse to leave Greece. At the same time she would leave Damien. She would stay in England and if he wanted her to continue to be his wife he would have to come and see her. Even then she would probably refuse to come back here with him.

It would be good to see Dick, good to see her mother too and repair the rift in their relationship. Maybe she would go back to work at Hayton's in the editorial department. She was tired already of the Sybaritic way of life she had to lead as Damien's wife. She was tired of coming to this island to be watched over by Stephanos every time Damien went away without her. She was bored with being a kept woman....

"Hi! This is a stroke of luck. I didn't expect to find you here. How are you, Teri? Blooming, by the looks of you."

The voice was Paul's, cheerful and mocking. Opening her eyes, Teri saw him, his shapely head silhouetted against the brilliance of the sun and was so glad to see him that she jumped up from the lounger to embrace him.

"Hey, steady on!" he said, laughing. "Step-Grandmother Melina is watching us, and you must know by now what a tell-tale she is. Last time I saw him Damien gave me hell all because she'd told him about our behaviour in and out of this pool last time we were both here."

"I don't care what she sees or what she tells him," Teri retorted. "What are you doing here? Last time I heard about you you were on your way back to the States, working as a deck-hand on the latest addition to the Nikerios freighter fleet.''

"That's right.'' Paul flung himself down on the other lounger. Dressed in close-fitting jeans and a blue T-shirt, he looked fit and sun-tanned. It was difficult to believe that at twenty he was only two years older than her brother, Teri thought. He looked so much more mature physically than Dick. But that was the Greek blood showing. He was probably much more experienced in sexual matters than Dick was, too, she decided wryly. "I have Damien to thank for that, too,'' he went on, his mouth curving ironically. "I guess he didn't like you and me going about together, so he had me removed while you were away on your honeymoon. Where is he now?''

"Gone to Saudi Arabia to negotiate with someone about the shipping of oil,'' she shrugged indifferently.

"Why aren't you with him?''

"I wasn't asked to go,'' she replied flatly. "How do you like going to sea?''

"It's damn hard work,'' he said. "But I can see why it's a good idea for me to get the experience if I'm to be an executive in the corporation one day.'' His grin flashed out. "At least that's the story I told Momma when I went to see her in New York. She sent a message to you, wished you all the best in your marriage to Damien. She's coming over later in the summer to visit Grandfather and her sister. I suppose you've met Aunt Katina and her daughters by now, and the rest of the Nikerios clan.''

"Katina threw a big party for us when we came back from the Aegean,'' Teri replied, "so that I could meet everyone.'' She made a face. "It was terrible,'' she added. "I felt like a prize possession on show.''

"I bet." Paul's glance was sympathetic. "But it seems to have done the trick, this marriage of Damien's. Grandfather is very taken with you. Damien must be priding himself on his own quickwittedness and good judgment." He sat up and leaned forward, his dark eyes staring at her intently. "Dust in the old man's eyes, that's what you are, Momma says," he said slowly.

"Whatever does she mean?"

"I'm not sure I should tell you," he replied tantalisingly, leaning back again, putting his hands behind his head and closing his eyes. "Mmm, it's good to be here for an hour or so, away from that devilish third mate."

"Tell me," Teri ordered imperiously. "Tell me what your mother meant!"

Paul opened one eye to look at her mockingly.

"I seem to remember you didn't like me to talk to you about Damien's relationship with Melina. You didn't want to know about it," he drawled tormentingly. "And I've no desire to get my ears boxed just for telling you the truth."

"What truth? Paul, will you stop tantalising! What did your mother mean?"

"Okay." He gave an exaggerated sigh. "When I told her about you she said she was surprised that Damien had married. He's always been such a loner and it was the last thing any member of the family had expected him to do. She could only think he'd got married to prevent Grandfather from tumbling to the truth that he and Melina are lovers."

"You're making this up," Teri protested.

"No, I'm not. Honest to God, Teri, it's what she said," he objected, sitting up again and leaning towards her earnestly. "And it fitted in so well with what I'd seen and overheard when I first arrived here in March that I couldn't help but believe what she said."

"What did you see and hear?" she asked woodenly.

"I saw what you've seen since you came here. I saw Melina hogging Damien's attention whenever he came here. I saw her take him off, presumably to her room, on the excuse that she had to talk to him about Grandfather's health. I've seen him going back to his own villa in the early hours of the morning after being with her, but what's more important, I overheard him and Grandfather quarrelling several times."

"About what?"

"Mostly about Damien's unmarried status, and one day Grandfather actually accused him of playing around with other men's wives, almost as if he'd guessed at the situation between Melina and Damien."

"What did Damien say?"

"He didn't deny it and defended his right to live his life as he wanted without interference. He was very bitter about it—and then Grandfather threw his bomb. He told Damien that if he didn't marry and produce an heir within the year he would not only cut him out of his will but would see to it personally that Damien was removed from his executive position in the Nikerios Corporation. Oh, I can tell you, Teri, it was high ding-dong here that afternoon, and in the end Damien slammed out in a fury and Grandfather took a fit of coughing and had to be put to bed. He was pretty miserable for a while, kept playing with his worry beads. I think he was afraid Damien had gone for good. His relief when he received a message from him saying he had got married in London and was bringing his new wife to Skios was pathetic." Paul paused, stared at her narrowly. "Still think I'm making it up?"

"No. No, I don't." Teri shook her head negatively,

avoiding his eyes. It all fitted in too well with what she knew and with what she had noticed herself since she had come to Greece. There had been times during the past few weeks when she had wondered why Damien had married in such a hurry a woman he had picked up in a gambling establishment. And now she knew that too.

"Teri, you're not hurt or anything?" Paul's voice expressed concern. "I mean, it isn't as if you and Damien married for love, is it?"

"No, I'm not hurt," she replied lightly. "Whew, it's getting too hot for me sitting out here, and I don't want to get scorched. How long are you staying here?"

"I've only come over for a few hours, just to see Grandfather and give him messages from Momma. I'm going back to Athens later this afternoon."

"I think I'll come with you," said Teri, swinging her legs off the lounger and standing up. She gave him her brightest smile. "That should give Melina something to tell tales about to Damien when he comes back, shouldn't it?"

"When is he coming back?" he asked, also getting to his feet.

"Oh, Thursday or Friday, I'm not too sure," she said casually, slipping her arm through his as they moved towards the house. Through one of the wide windows which overlooked the pool area she had noticed Melina hovering and spying. "I'm so glad you've come, Paul," she went on, raising her voice as they stepped into the cool passageway inside the house, knowing her voice would carry to the pricked ears further along. "We can have fun together again in the next couple of days. Remember the night we danced in the Plaka?"

Everything worked out as Teri planned it. She re-

turned to Athens, managed by pleading a sick head-
ache to avoid going out on the town that evening with
Paul and next day booked a one-way ticket on a plane
to London. By the time Damien returned from Saudi
Arabia she would be gone. Her mind working clearly
and coldly, she wrote a letter to him telling him exactly why she was leaving him.

"Knowing now your reasons for acquiring a wife I
find I can no longer live with you," she wrote. "I had
not known a son could treat his father in such a cold
and calculating way. I find you despicable in every
way, and so I am leaving you, to give you the chance
to divorce me according to the agreement which we
signed. I hope I never see you again, so please do not
attempt to follow me."

After receiving such a letter he wouldn't make any
attempt to cajole her into staying with her, she was sure.
He was too proud for that and she had no regrets about
leaving him—at least not yet, she thought as the plane
took off and she watched the jumble of futuristic buildings and ancient edifices which was Athens slide away
under the wing. And there were some people who
would be very pleased she had walked out on him. Melina for one. Her mother for another.

She had to admit to feeling a little apprehensive
when at last she arrived at the house in Richmond. Suppose her mother refused to see her? Suppose she was
turned away? But one look at Bridget's face when she
opened the door and she knew she had worried unduly.

"Teri, oh Teri, I'm so glad to see you!" Bridget exclaimed, and flinging her arms about her daughter
burst into tears.

"I shouldn't have said what I did to you on the
phone that day," she said later as they sat together in
the big lounge with its comfortable rather shabby arm-

chairs, its shelves loaded with books and its two long Regency-style windows overlooking a lawn which swept down to the River Thames. "I've often regretted it. It was such a shock, you see, hearing you'd married so suddenly and for such a reason."

"I realised that at the time," Teri replied comfortingly. "But Damien was in such a hurry and I had to tell you what I'd done and where I was going. Anyway, it's all over now."

"Over?" Bridget looked bewildered and then her expression changed slowly and became one of exasperation. It was an expression Teri had often seen on her mother's face before when Bridget guessed that either her husband Alex or her daughter had done something wildly impulsive and illogical. "Now what have you done?" she groaned, leaning against the cretonne-covered back of the deep armchair in which she was sitting.

"I've left him," said Teri, getting to her feet and striding over to the window, hands dug deep in the slit pockets of her skirt suit. It was twilight and between the trunks and trailing branches of the willows which lined the river she could see the water shining like silver. Stars were beginning to twinkle in the sky. What time would it be in Greece? She made a rapid calculation. Damien would be back now, on Skios, talking with Melina—or sleeping with her? Jealousy clawed suddenly in her breast and she drew a sharp breath.

"Left whom? Not... not your husband?" Bridget sounded plaintive.

"Yes, I've left Damien." Teri spoke coldly and flatly, as she leaned her hot forehead against the cool pane of the window.

"But you've only been married.:..." Bridget broke off, obviously calculating silently.

"Two and a half months," put in Teri. "I didn't intend to leave him quite so soon," she went on explaining. "I was going to stick it out for longer, at least a year, but...but..." her voice quavered in spite of herself, "when I found out how unbearable being married to him was going to be I took the first opportunity to fly home."

"Unbearable? What do you mean? Teri, you're not saying that he...he's one of those men who take pleasure in being cruel to women, are you?" Bridget's blue eyes were round and horrified.

"No, oh no," Teri found she was laughing a little. "There was nothing like that. In fact he was very kind to me, very generous."

"Then why?"

"Mother, you know why I married him," Teri said impatiently. "For the money which he lent to father and which is now in Hayton's. I knew it wouldn't last forever, that it was just a convenience marriage and that one day it would end. I'm precipitating the end, that's all, by leaving him now."

"And has he agreed to this? He's agreed to separation."

"I don't know. I didn't wait to ask him, but I think he will."

"It's all very puzzling," Bridget shook her head, her fingers teasing her grey blonde hair. "Are you sure, Teri, you haven't broken the contract you signed by leaving him?"

"I may have done," Teri felt suddenly exhausted. "I don't know. It remains to be seen." She paused, then whispered to the window-pane. "I couldn't stay, knowing why he'd married me, I couldn't stay when I found out what he had done."

"I do wish you'd be more explicit," Bridget complained. "How on earth you expect me to understand your behaviour when you talk in such a vague way I don't know. I have to tell you, Teri, I'm not surprised this has happened. You didn't marry for love. If you loved this man you wouldn't have left him just because he'd done something you don't like."

"I've left him because I've found out he married me to cover up an affair he's been having with his father's third wife," Teri said between her teeth as she swung round to glare at her mother. "Could you have stayed with a man who'd done that, even if you loved him?" she demanded.

"Oh, my God!" exclaimed Bridget in horrified tones. "It's worse than one of those awful Greek tragedies your father was so fond of going to see at the theatre."

"No, not worse than, but nearly as bad as, or it could be if it was allowed to develop," replied Teri unable to keep from smiling at her mother's comparison. "But I couldn't stay to be a party to a deception of an old man, even if he is a devious, fraudulent old devil who's become wealthy by stepping on other people and cheating them."

"No, you're quite right, you couldn't," agreed Bridget forcibly. "We aren't that sort of people and we don't really want to be associated with such people." She shuddered slightly. "I can't understand yet how Alex came to be involved with the Nikerios family. Yes, you were right to come home, Teri. I can only hope that man won't come and entangle you in his affair again."

"Somehow I don't think he will."

And she was right. Damien didn't follow her nor did he write to her directly. Only through Mr. Fenton, the lawyer who had drawn up the contract, did she hear from him and the message she received relieved her mind somewhat. He had received her letter and would abide by her decision not to return to Greece and he would not follow her or come to see her unless she actually invited him to come. He had asked Mr. Fenton to arrange for the payment of her allowance into her bank in London, hoping that would be agreeable to her.

"And the contract?" Teri said hesitantly. "The one we signed before we were married? Does that still stand?"

"Mr. Nikerios made no mention of it," replied Mr. Fenton in his frigid way, giving her a disapproving glance. "I suppose you're wondering about his investment in Hayton's?"

"Yes, I am," she said stiffly, hating the humiliating position in which she found herself.

"You're quite safe." The lawyer said with just the slightest suspicion of a sneer. "Obviously, you don't remember but there is a clause covering a situation like this. In the event of a separation or a complete break-up of the marriage Mr. Nikerios will have no right to insist on the payment of the debt incurred by your father. Does that clear the matter up for you?"

Teri nodded, feeling her cheeks flame with unusual colour under his ironic gaze. Mr. Fenton was making it very clear whose side he was on.

Next day she went to Hayton's to see Harry Cogswell, her former boss in the editorial department, and to ask for her job back.

"No can do," he told her. "Filled your position as soon as you left. A chap by the name of Hackett, straight out of Oxford. Good, too."

"Better than I am?" she rallied him.

"Much better." He stared at her narrowly. "Marriage come apart at the seams already?" he jibed.

"Yes. I wouldn't be looking for a job otherwise, would I?" she countered.

"You should worry. The Damien Nikerioses of this world can afford to keep several ex-wives, mistresses too," he jeered.

"That isn't the problem, Harry," she argued, keeping to herself the fact that she had no intention of touching the money Damien would pay into her account. "I want to work. I missed working when I left here. Can't you squeeze me in somewhere? After all, I do own shares in the company."

"All right. Give me a few days to think about it. I'll get back to you."

It was the end of June before he did. By then she had been with her mother to Brookhill Sports Day and had seen Dick cover himself in glory by winning both his races. He seemed very disappointed when she told him she had decided to separate from Damien.

"Oh, you would," he growled at her. "I was hoping to meet him and have a holiday in Greece on that island you were staying on."

"I'm sorry," she replied stiffly, wondering why she felt suddenly sick and giddy.

Several times that week the sickness and giddiness attacked her and in a state of panic she made an appointment at a hospital clinic for an examination, not wanting to visit the family doctor. At the clinic it was confirmed that she was going to have a baby. What she had been determined to avoid had happened and she had no one to blame but herself. Without telling her mother or anyone else about this new problem she visited other doctors and clinics during the next few days and after listening to their advice and going through several harassing days and nights struggling with her conscience decided that there was nothing she could do to change her condition.

She wasn't going to tell Damien, though, she thought determinedly. He would come and take the child away from her as soon as it was born if she did, because it was written into the contract that he was to have the custody of any child born to them. She knew now why he had insisted on that condition.

It would have to be kept a secret right up to the time of the birth. She would have to go into hiding somewhere, find a job in the country. But how and where? Every day she scanned the advertisements in the newspapers hoping to find a job which would suit her purpose. Surely someone wanted a housekeeper for a country house or castle in the wilds of Scotland or Wales? Surely someone was looking for a nanny to mind young children? Or did that sort of job exist only in her imagination?

At last Harry Cogswell phoned.

"Ever heard of Miles Trinton?" he asked.

"Yes. He 's a leading classicist. We published a book of his some years ago."

"Right. He's in the process of working on another, tracing the influence of the Greek myths on literature through the ages, but he needs help with the indexing and footnotes or he's going to be behind schedule. Interested in helping him? It would mean living in his home, somewhere in Scotland, for a few months, probably until Christmas. And you needn't worry about the proprieties of the idea. His wife is all for it, especially when I told her you're Alex's daughter."

"I'm interested, Harry," Teri told him. "How soon do they want me?"

"Immediately. Got a pen there? I'll give you the address and you can get in touch personally."

Teri wrote at once to Miles Trinton—and by return of post was offered the job.

Hardly able to believe her good luck, Teri set off three days later for Dumfries. She went by train and was met at the end of her journey by Helen Trinton, a pink-cheeked, grey-haired woman who was wearing a well-cut suit of heather-coloured tweed and was accompanied by her two golden Labradors.

"We haven't met before, but I feel I've known you ever since you were born," she said as she drove the car she had come in out of the station yard. "Alex was always talking about you. He was such a good friend to us and we were so sorry when he was killed. I wrote to your mother with our condolences."

"Yes, so she said," murmured Teri, "when I mentioned to her that I was coming to stay with you." She looked out at the street along which they were passing. The houses were all built of red sandstone which looked dark and dreary in the misty rain which was falling. "Do we have far to go to your house?"

"About twenty miles. It's on the coast. It was my father's family home and used to be a farm. When Dad died he left it to me and Miles and I use it as a holiday place in the summer and other times. Of course, since he's been working on this book we've been living there all the time. I think you'll like it."

"Is Dumfries the nearest town?" asked Teri.

"Of any size, yes."

"Is there a hospital here?" They were passing a statue now, set in front of a church with a tall spire. "Oh, who's that?" Teri added inconsequently.

"Robbie Burns, of course. He used to live here, you know, in a cottage along a street in that direction." Helen changed gear as they approached some traffic lights. "And yes, there is a hospital. Why do you ask?"

"I like to know what facilities there are available," Teri replied casually.

The car moved forward over a bridge and then climbed a hill.

"This is Maxwelltown where Annie Laurie is supposed to have lived," said Helen. "You'll find that the whole district is teeming with literary and historical associations. Not far from Auchenbriggs—that's our house— is Kirbean where John Paul Jones was born. He's credited with being the founder of the American Navy, you know."

Her soft sing-song Scottish voice droned on, but Teri didn't listen very closely as she looked out at the misty grey hills. Everything was grey and indistinct, so different from Greece. Even the whitewashed cottages of a small hamlet looked grey. Would they ever dazzle the eyes in bright sunlight like the cube-like houses did on Skios; like her own house in Athens did? Her hand clenched slowly on her lap and she chewed at her lower lip. Oh God, she had forgotten about the house! What would happen to it now? Would Damien put it up for sale and send her the proceeds?

The car turned off along a winding road which dipped up and down hill and after a while she began to feel sick. She was just thinking of asking Helen Trinton to stop and let her out to breathe in some fresh air when the car swung in through a gateway and crunched up a driveway. It came to a stop at the top of a rise in front of a long low cottage from whose windows lights were already gleaming.

Miles Trinton was a tall, thin man with a scholar's stoop. He gave Teri a sharp assessing look when he shook hands with her and exclaimed, "My God, you look green! Feeling sick?"

"A little. I'll be all right."

"It's the way Helen drives along the road. She doesn't know the meaning of slow, takes most bends on two wheels," he said with a smile. "So you're Alex's daughter. You must know, my dear, we're awfully glad to have you here."

It didn't take long for Teri to settle down, they both made her so comfortable and welcome. She had a small bedroom under the eaves of the cottage with a dormer window which had a view of the Solway Firth. It was furnished simply but pleasantly with old pinewood furniture and if she wanted to be alone she could sit up there.

The situation of the cottage was delightful. Sitting over the top of a low hill, it was surrounded by overgrown fields which at that time of the year were full of daisies and buttercups, poppies and cornflowers. The fields sloped down to the foot of the hills and the coast road and beyond the road was a narrow shingly beach eddying the silvery waters of the firth.

Once she had started work the days passed swiftly and pleasantly. Mostly the weather was good that summer, with many clear days when the sea sparkled under pale blue skies. When she wasn't working Teri took long walks, sometimes with Helen and the dogs, sometimes alone. When the period of sickness passed she began to feel very well and could see a change in herself. Her cheeks glowed, her eyes sparkled. She looked better than she had ever looked in her life.

Sometimes she wondered how long she would be able to keep the fact that she was pregnant from the Trintons, and as July gave way to August and she felt the baby kick within her she knew she would have to visit a doctor or a hospital clinic soon to make arrangements for the delivery of the baby. The difficulty in arranging such a visit to Dumfries without alerting Helen to the truth seemed insurmountable to her, so one morning at breakfast she decided to tell them. They were astonished.

"But we didn't even know you were married!" Helen exclaimed. "You don't wear a ring."

"It's here." Teri put her hand to the opening of her blouse and slipped out the thin chain of gold which Damien had given her and on which she had slung the ring when she had left him.

"And where is your husband? What's his name?" Helen went on. Miles, it seemed, was still too stunned by the news to ask questions.

"He...we...we're separated," Teri confessed.

"He knows about the child, though." Miles spoke at last, his glance in her direction sharp.

"No. I don't want him to know. I...I...haven't told anyone about the baby, not even my mother, and I'd be glad if you would also keep it to yourselves," said Teri. "I've only told you now because it's due to be born in December and I'll have to go to the hospital soon to make sure everything is all right. You see, I'll still be working here when it comes...at least," she licked dry lips, "that is if you still want me to stay."

"Of course we want you to stay," said Helen. "Miles can't finish that book in time without your help. But I do think...." She paused, looking a little embarrassed. "I feel very impertinent asking you this, Teri, but your husband is the father of the baby, isn't he?"

"Yes."

"Then I think you should tell him."

"No, I can't. I won't!" Teri's voice rose excitedly. "He'll take the baby from me when it's born if I do."

"Good God! What sort of a monster is he?" gasped Helen.

It all came out then. She told them everything about Alex's debt, her own foolish gambling, the contract with Damien and her reasons for leaving him. They listened attentively and patiently, not interrupting her once, drawing their own conclusions from the way her face changed and her voice softened whenever she spoke of Damien.

"Mmm, interesting," Miles murmured. "It's a pity you didn't stay to ask him if what that young Paul told you was true. A man has a right to defend himself, you know, and is never guilty until proved to be so. However, it's done now and you can depend on us to respect your confidence."

"But supposing something goes wrong, at the last minute, I mean?" Helen said practically. "First babies often have a way of being awkward. You should give us permission to let someone know if you're ill."

"Only my mother. You could inform her, but only if it's absolutely necessary."

"She should really know beforehand," protested Helen. "So that it doesn't come as too much of a shock. She should know you're going to have a child so that she'll be prepared."

"All right," Teri sighed. "I'll write to her nearer to time."

"And afterwards, after the baby is born, what then?" asked Helen.

"I don't know." Teri's smile had some of its usual reckless quality. "I'll face that when I come to it."

CHAPTER SIX

On a day near the end of December Teri was taken into the hospital for a Caesarean operation. It had been recommended by the gynecologist who had been examining her during the final stages of her pregnancy.

"You're a wee bit too narrow for this job," he had said, echoing Stephanos's words, "and it will be for your benefit and the baby's."

And although anxious, because having come so far she did not want to lose Damien's child, Teri had agreed to have the operation performed. As a result she came round from the anaesthetic one sunny frosty morning to be told by a nurse that she was the mother of a 'fine wee laddie' with a good pair of lungs and a great appetite.

They put the baby in a cot beside the bed in the small single ward where she lay half dozing, recovering from the operation. Heaving herself up in the bed, grimacing at the pain caused by the stitches down her middle which were pulling at her skin, Teri looked down at him. He seemed to be all right and was sleeping again, both tiny fists up near his mouth.

How dark he was, like Damien, with a dusky golden skin and lustrous black hair contrasting sharply with the white sheets of the cot. Damien would have no doubts that the child was his son... if he ever saw him.

She lay down again and stared at the ceiling. She

had come through her ordeal. She had shown she had stamina and had survived. She wished, for some reason, that Stephanos Nikerios could know that she had. She wished Damien could know. But how could either of them know if she didn't tell them?

Tears of weakness gathered in her eyes and slid down her cheeks. The pride which had kept her going during the past months and which had enabled her to suppress any feelings of softness towards Damien was suddenly in the dust. What had she done? Why had she kept from him the news that she was going to have his child? And what right had she to deprive the child of his father? Oh, how she wished Damien would come and share with her this lovely boy whom they had made together. She had been wanting him to come for months now, hoping secretly that he would ignore her imperious order that he was not to follow her, longing for him to appear out of the blue and carry her off to Greece, to anywhere as long as she was with him.

"Och now, what's the matter with ye?" A nurse had come into the room to check on the baby. "Feeling sorry for yeself?"

"I'd like Damien to know about the baby," Teri whispered. "I'd like him to come and see him."

"And who is Damien?" asked the nurse casually, taking Teri's limp wrist between her cool fingers, searching for the pulse and looking at her watch meanwhile.

"My...my...husband, the baby's father."

"I expect he'll be coming at visiting time," said the nurse indifferently.

"No, he won't." Teri was suddenly urgent, raising her head from the pillow. "You see, he doesn't live in this country and he'll only come if I ask him." She fell back against the pillow, feeling weak again, and the tears streamed down her face. "Oh, I do want him to come. I do want him!"

The nurse released her wrist and straightened the bedclothes, her narrow face completely expressionless.

"Now listen, the best thing you can do is sleep," she said briskly. "Your pulse is far too fast and ye won't get well if ye don't rest, then who will look after the baby? Ye have someone else to think about as well as yeself now, you know. I see he hasn't got a name yet. Ye might be thinking of one for him. Any ideas?"

"What's the date today?" whispered Teri, wiping the tears from her cheeks with her fingers, already regretting having given way before a stranger.

"My goodness, ye are in a bad way if ye've forgotten the date ye had to come in. It's December twenty-seven, so it is, and the baby was delivered this morning at nine o'clock."

The twenty-seventh, one day after Stephanos's birthday, who had been given his name, so he had told her, because he had been born on St. Stephen's Day.

"I think I'd like to call him Steph...Stephen," Teri whispered, and the nurse smiled and nodded.

"Good for you," she said. "Now you're beginning to think positively."

Since they were both fundamentally healthy Teri and Stephen made good progress and were allowed to leave the hospital at the end of two weeks. Miles and Helen came to collect them and drove them both back to Auchenbriggs where Helen had arranged the cot Teri had bought, in a small boxroom next to the bedroom which Teri used.

There were letters and gifts from Bridget and Dick waiting for Teri, but from no one else. Nothing from Damien. But why should there be anything from him? He didn't know. She hadn't asked anyone to tell him. Only in that moment of weakness after the operation had she told a nurse whom she hadn't seen again. Presumably that nurse hadn't told anyone else either. And why should she? She had probably assumed that Teri would have visitors who would take care of spreading the news of the baby's birth to whomever it concerned.

Keeping to herself her deep disappointment, telling herself that she had only wanted Damien to come and see her while she had been feeling weak, Teri settled down to helping Miles finish the book and to the caring of Stephen. By the end of January the manuscript was fully indexed and the footnotes had been completed. It was ready for the publisher and it was agreed that the Trintons would drive down to London to deliver it personally to the editors at Hayton's, taking Teri and Stephen with them. Teri phoned her mother saying she would be coming to stay with her in Richmond for a while. Beyond that she hadn't planned.

On the afternoon before the day of their departure from Scotland, Teri decided to pack up some of her clothing while Stephen was taking his afternoon nap in his pram which she had parked in the back porch, leaving the door open so that he would get the benefit of the clear fresh air on that mild sunny day. Helen had gone into Dumfries on some last-minute errands and Miles was somewhere about, possibly also preparing for the next day's journey.

Teri had to admit she was packing in a very desultory way. The view from the bedroom window kept distracting her. Visibility was so good she could see

the mountains of the Lake District on the other side
of the Firth, peaks of silver and violet faintly etched
against a pale blue sky. In the Firth itself the tide was
out, revealing stretches of smooth, shining brown
mud.

"Teri?" There was a knock on the door and Miles'
voice called her name. He sounded slightly breathless.
"Are you there?"

"Yes? What is it? Is Stephen crying?" she went over
to the door and opened it. Miles, looking flushed, and
behind his thick-lensed spectacles his grey eyes had a
sparkle of excitement, most unusual for him.

"No. At least I don't think so. I haven't heard
him," he replied. "You have a visitor."

"Oh? Who is it?" She supposed it was one of the
neighbours whom she had met during her stay at Auchenbriggs, come to see the baby and perhaps offer
him a small gift, as was the custom.

"You'll see. Just come downstairs," said Miles
mysteriously, and went away down the landing.

Puzzled by his behaviour, Teri went back into the
room to glance at herself in the long mirror and made
sure she was presentable. Since Stephen had been
born she had been wearing her hair drawn back from
her forehead as usual, but instead of letting it cascade
to her shoulders in a wild tangle of ringlets she had
been winding it into a knot on top of her head. It
wasn't always a very neat arrangement because it
would keep escaping to hang down in surprisingly attractive wisps about her ears and the back of her neck,
giving the impression that though she tried hard to
discipline herself she was still inclined to be impulsive
and given to mercurial changes of mind.

But the style did make her look a little more mature, she thought, and she had more shape too, her

glance roving critically over her figure. Both were shown off by the sweater dress she was wearing of ribbed wool. Beige and brown in colour, it had a close-fitting turtle neck, an A-shaped skirt and was belted at the waist with a wide tan leather belt decorated with brass studs.

Quickly Teri took off her slippers and stepped into high-heeled beige shoes. She outlined her lips with beige shiny lipstick, made sure her eyes were made up correctly, flicked powder across her nose and satisfied that she looked calm and collected as she imagined a working mother should look, she went downstairs and into the living room.

There was no one in the comfortable cream and blue room except the dogs. They were sprawled on the hearthrug obviously resting after a run with Miles and they didn't even move when she entered. She crossed the hall to the dining room. No one there. On to the kitchen she went. The door to the porch was slightly open and through it she could see a dark figure bending over the pram. Someone was about to steal Stephen!

Rushing forward, Teri flung back the door and ran into the porch, ready to seize hold of the intruder and do battle for her son.

"What are you doing? Leave him alone!" she commanded, and then felt all the breath go out of her, her throat close up and her heart begin to pound excitedly as she recognised the man who was straightening up and turning to look at her. "Damien!" she croaked. "What are you doing here?"

Hands deep in the trouser pockets of his charcoal grey business suit, he flicked her a seemingly disinterested glance, then turned back to look down at the sleeping child, bending forward over the pram.

"He looks like me," he murmured, and there was a note of surprise in his voice. "I've always believed babies look like babies and bear no resemblance to anyone else, no matter what their mothers and their grandmothers say, but I can see that this one looks like me."

"Of course he does. He's your child," she blurted out.

"Really?" There was insolence now in the cool lilt of his voice and also in the glance he directed at her.

"Really!" Teri raged. Already this meeting with him wasn't going at all as she imagined a meeting with him might go. He wasn't behaving at all like a domineering husband should. He hadn't swept her into his arms and kissed her breathlessy and demanded his marital rights. "Who else's child could he be?"

"He could be Paul's," Damien drawled, giving her a slitted, dangerously glittering look.

"Oh!" Teri was so furious she couldn't speak. Going right up to him, she slapped his cheek as hard as she could and turning round marched back into the house. She was half way up the stairs when she realised she had left him alone with Stephen and he could kidnap the child, had the cool nerve to carry the baby off to Greece without even asking her permission, so she began to run down the stairs again, only to find him standing at the bottom of the staircase, arms folded across his chest, watching her from under those wicked, devilish eyebrows.

Collecting herself together, she walked down the last few stairs in a slow dignified way, her eyelids drooping haughtily as her eyes met his black inimical stare. But she could not step off the last stair because he was in the way. Eyes on a level, they glared at each other and Teri caught her lower lip between her teeth when she saw the marks her hand had made on Damien's lean cheek.

"Why?" she faltered. "Why did you say that? Why did you think he might be Paul's?"

"From all accounts you and he were very friendly when you were staying on Skios and I was away," he replied, his mouth taking on a cynical curve. "Even the last time he was there you went back to Athens with him. Then you left and said in your note you didn't want to see me any more." His shoulders lifted in a shrug. "I drew my own conclusions about you and him."

Teri stared at him in stunned silence, as she realised what conclusions Damien could have drawn from her own reckless behaviour. But only if someone had told him about Paul and herself. Only if someone had insinuated that there had been more than a light-hearted friendship in their brief association. Who could have done that? Not Stephanos, she was sure of that. He had wanted her to stay with Damien too much. Who could it have been? Paul himself? Or Melina?

"How did you know where to find me?" she asked slowly.

"I asked Fenton and he gave me this address." Again his glance was insolent as it swept over her. "You're living with that man, the one who let me in?" he drawled.

The implication was clear, hurting her unbearably as he indicated how he regarded her, as a woman who slept around.

"I've been working for him" she said between set teeth, and pushing past him at last went into the living room. "And if you don't believe me you'd better stay and ask his wife Helen when she comes back from

Dumfries," she added, swinging round to face him as he followed her into the room.

"What sort of work?" he asked.

"Indexing, footnotes for his book, making sure all the acknowledgements are made for quotations he'd used from other writers' works. It's finished now and we're all going to London tomorrow. I'll be going to Richmond to stay with my mother for a while," she said coolly, drifting over to one of the windows. It looked out on to the driveway. In front of the doorway a sleek black car was parked. "Did you drive all the way here?" she asked politely.

"I did." He came to stand on the other side of the window, leaning a shoulder against the wall. "It was interesting. I have never seen anything of England beyond London before. It is a beautiful country. Nor have I ever been to Scotland." There was a brief awkward silence. "You look different," he added.

Teri half turned to look at him. To her he seemed just the same—dark-haired, olive-skinned, beaky-nosed, handsome in a satanic way. Their eyes met, something glowing in the black depths of his.

"You look very well," he said softly. "Motherhood becomes you."

Her eyes widened briefly, warily, and her glance skittered away from his out to the garden where dead grasses and the dried-up remains of wild flowers took on a reddish glow from the sunlight.

"Did someone tell you...about the baby?" she asked. "Did someone ask you to come and see me?"

"No. No one asked me to come and no one told me about the baby until I arrived here just now when Miles—is that what you called him?—let me in. He said he supposed I'd like to have a look at the baby while I was waiting for you to come down and directed me to the porch. Teri, why didn't you let me know you were pregnant?''

"I...er...." Again she gave him a quick, wary glance and looked away again. "I don't know," she muttered. "You see, I wasn't sure...." Her voice faltered and she bit her lip, not sure how much she should tell him now.

"You weren't sure it was mine, perhaps?" Damien's voice was dry.

"No...no...not that. I was sure it was yours. You see, there's never been anyone else. In spite of what you believed about Paul and me we didn't...." She broke off again and swung round on him. "Oh, you had no right to suggest it was Paul's!" she flared. "No right at all...." Once more her voice faded when she saw mockery glinting in his eyes and curving his mouth.

"I had to find out somehow if the child was mine, since you had seen fit not to inform me of his birth," he put in, still with a touch of bitterness. "Your reactions have convinced me that he is." His fingers touched his cheek briefly. "You hit hard, Teri."

"Oh, I'm sorry," she cried. "I didn't mean to hurt you." An urge to move towards him to reach up and kiss his cheek almost overwhelmed her. Hands at her own cheeks, she forced herself to keep looking out at the garden. "Then if no one asked you to come, why have you come?" she said.

Again there was an awkward silence, Teri heard Damien move away and looking round watched him pace over to the fireplace. The two dogs, sensing an alien presence, opened sleepy eyes and growled softly. At once Damien squatted down and offered one of them a fist to sniff at, then began to ruffle the hair at their necks. Both animals stretched lazily, liking such treatment.

"My father is very ill," he said at last, rising to his feet and turning to her. "He is dying."

"I'm sorry," she said again, her voice without life. He hadn't come because he had wanted to see her, because he wanted her back. He hadn't come because he loved her. "Surely you could have written to tell me that. Or sent a message through Mr. Fenton," she added coldly, trying to cover up the hurt she was feeling.

"And what would you have done if I had written to tell you? Sent back a note of apology and condolence? Said you're sorry in your polite, frigid English way?" he grated, and stepped across to her, the Greek fire of his anger leaping up suddenly, flaming out to scorch her. There was a savage hissing sound as he drew in his breath and visibly controlled himself. "I came myself to tell you and to ask you to come back to Skios with me, to end our separation for a while... at least until he dies." He drew another deep breath. "He would like to see you, has asked for you often enough," he went on, his mouth softening. "He will be delighted when he knows about the child and will want to see him too. Will you come with me tomorrow instead of going with these friends of yours?"

The feeling of disappointment was being swamped now by a rippling tide of loathing because he could be so devious. He wanted his father to see Stephen to show the old man he had done what he had been asked to do; he had married and produced a son, so there would be no need for Stephanos to leave the bulk of his fortune elsewhere.

"I'll have to think about it," she said woodenly, and turned to look out of the window again, hearing gravel crunched under the wheels. Around the bend in the drive came the Trintons' car.

"And how long will it take you to *think*?" Damien drawled with a touch of irony. "From what I know of you you don't usually bother but act on the spur of the moment. Or perhaps I should say react." His breath hissed again. "All right, *think* about it. I'll stay the night somewhere. Presumably there is a village pub hereabouts. But I'll be going back to London early in the morning. I'll call here on my way and you can tell me what you have decided then."

Still standing at the window, Teri watched Helen taking parcels out of the car. Miles appeared, to help carry them, and together they walked towards the front door, pausing by the shiny black car while presumably Miles explained about it. They looked what they were—an amiable middle-aged couple who had grown closer over the years of their marriage, not apart; who understood each other and accepted each other. Looking at them, Teri couldn't imagine that they had ever gone through the experience she and Damien were going through now, this loving and hating at the same time, this wanting and rejecting.

"Teri, it will only be for a short time, perhaps two weeks. He can't last much longer." Damien's voice was soft and deep, shaken a little with some emotion, and his hands were gentle on her shoulders, smoothing them caressingly. Teri whirled at once.

"Please don't touch me," she whispered. "I...I can't bear you to touch me!"

All colour fled from his face, and his mouth thinned. He shoved his hands into his trouser pockets. Between narrowed lids his eyes hated her and she saw what she hadn't noticed before, a hollowness in his cheeks, lines of strain about his mouth, a bruised look beneath his eyes.

"I'll come," she said, suddenly making up her

mind. "I'll come with you tomorrow and go to Skios to see your father. But it's for his sake I'm coming and for no other reason. And... and you're not to take advantage of my coming. Do you understand?"

Dark lashes drifted down over his eyes and his mouth tightened even more. When he spoke it was stiffly.

"I understand."

And just then Helen and Miles came into the room.

They made no secret of their pleasure in having Damien in their house because he was Teri's husband. Thoroughly traditional in their outlook and behaviour, they believed in marriage and neither of them would hear of him going to stay the night in the small hotel in the nearby village.

"But of course you must stay here," insisted Helen. "It'll be no trouble. We have another bedroom. With a double bed in it, too." Her eyes twinkled as she looked across at Miles in a conspiratorial way. "I'll go and make it up. It's so wonderful to hear that you and Teri are going to be together again!"

And so Damien stayed to watch Teri as she attended to Stephen when the baby awoke and to walk with her along the road when she pushed the pram in the direction of the village. As they wandered beside the shore Teri had the curious feeling she was walking in a dream. It was all so different from anything else they had done together, so far away from the passionate physical abandonment they had experienced during their honeymoon among the sun-gilded, sea-girt Aegean islands. Yet the product of their passion was lying there contentedly in the pram and Damien's hand was resting on the pram's handle in a proprietorial way as he helped her push it up the hill.

When they returned to the house he helped her to prepare Stephen for bed and seemed to find pleasure in holding the baby, taking the child from her when she had finished feeding him and holding him against his shoulder to soothe him while she prepared the cot. The sight of her baby being held so confidently and comfortingly by those strong dark hands caused jealousy to twist through Teri and, remembering that Damien had the right to take custody of Stephen if she ever left him again and divorced him, she almost snatched the child from him.

The feeling of unreality she had experienced when she had been out walking came over her again as she sat at the table with Damien and the Trintons for the evening meal. Was it really possible that Damien Nikerios, erstwhile playboy and heir to millions, was sitting in that simple room eating plain wholesome Scottish food while conversing pleasantly and intelligently with two highly intellectual people about subjects of which she had imagined he would have been ignorant?

As usual she fed Stephen when he awoke about ten o'clock and when she returned to the living room she found Damien alone, the Trintons having gone to bed, he said, because they wanted to be up early in the morning to start the journey south.

"We'll go the same way they do," he decided, closing the map book he had been studying, "through the Lake District and down through Lancashire and Cheshire, to Oxford. That way we'll be able to get to Richmond without going through London."

"Mother will be surprised to see you," Teri commented.

"I suppose she will, but it's about time she and I met, isn't it? I'm sorry I can't take you and Stephen to meet my mother, but she is always away this time of the year, in the Bahamas," he replied. Leaning against the back of the couch where he was sitting he surveyed her through narrowed lids. "Looking after the baby must make you tired," he said. "Don't you think you should go to bed now, too?"

"Yes. But I'm not sleeping with you," she said sharply. "Stephen is only just a month old and... and... the doctor said that I shouldn't... at least not until six weeks is up."

"It's all right. You needn't think up excuses," he retorted, and rising to his feet and picking up his discarded suit jacket he slung it over one shoulder. "I'm quite used to sleeping by myself. Goodnight," he added coldly, and went from the room leaving Teri feeling as if he had just slapped her face as she had slapped his earlier.

The journey next day went surprisingly smoothly. Stephen proved he was an exceptionally good traveller by sleeping quite contentedly in his carrycot on the back seat of the car, only waking to be fed. At first the weather was good and as they swept along the highway which cuts through the dark fells of Cumbria they were able to see moorland sunlit and shadowed, stretching for miles away to the distant curves and peaks of mountains and hills.

Teri found it impossible to drive such a long way without talking and so she asked Damien questions about his father and eventually he opened up, telling her about Stephanos's sudden collapse not long after she had left Skios, of the operations which had been performed during the summer months on various parts of his digestive system, of how Damien had even taken him to New York where he could benefit from the attention of some of the best surgeons in the world.

"But it was no use," he said. "And in November he asked me to bring him home, back to Skios—he said he wanted to die there and be buried there." He shrugged his shoulders. "All I have done the past few months is make sure that his every whim is granted if possible, that he has had everything he desires during these last few weeks." He slanted her a sidelong glance. "That is why I came for you, as I've told you."

Teri didn't say anything for a while, but sat looking out as the road dipped down to the Lancashire plain, seeing only vaguely distant chimneys pointing upwards under lowering grey clouds which were sweeping inland, blown from the sea by a strong westerly wind. Listening to Damien talking about his father, hearing the occasional quiver of emotion in the smooth flow of his deep voice, it was easy to believe that at heart he was a very compassionate person who wanted only to please his father because he loved him. It was easy to forget that he was probably only pleasing the old man because of the threat Stephanos had once uttered and about which Paul had told her.

But she mustn't forget how cunning he was. She mustn't forget why he had married her. And above all she mustn't forget why he had at last come for her. It wasn't because he loved her and needed her, and she was to stay with him only as long as Stephanos lived.

By the time they were bypassing Birmingham rain had begun to fall, and it seemed that with the change in the weather Stephen had become restless. Only when Teri took him on her knee to nurse him did he stop crying, and by the time the car turned down the road where her mother lived Teri was feeling tired and her nerves were stretched to breaking point.

Stephen was roaring lustily when Bridget opened

the front door. At once she took the baby from Teri's arms.

"Ah, poor poppet," she crooned taking him into the house. "What have they been doing to you? Did you want your supper, then? Well, you shall have it." She turned round. "Teri—" she began imperiously, saw Damien behind Teri and stared.

"Mother, this is Damien," said Teri hurriedly. "He...I...well, we're going to Greece tomorrow, to see his father and...."

"You might have let me know, darling, that you were ending your separation," Bridget chided her. Surprisingly Stephen had now stopped roaring, much to Teri's irritation, who wondered why it was he stopped crying when someone else held him but wouldn't stop for her. His head rested comfortably against his grandmother's shoulder and he was sucking his own fist. "I'm Bridget Hayton," continued Bridget, smiling at Damien. "It's about time you and I met, don't you think?"

Her words, the same Damien had used the previous night to Teri, seemed to amuse him. He gave her his slow crooked smile and with a feeling compounded of frustration and resignation Teri watched her mother capitulate to its warm charm. It was irritating too, later, to watch how easily Damien conquered her brother Dick who was now working at Hayton's. Most of the evening Dick monopolised Damien's attention, talking about running, and for the first time she learned a little of what her husband had done when he had been a young man as he described some of his experiences when representing his country in various amateur athletic meetings.

"He's much different from what I had expected," Bridget said in the kitchen as she prepared bedtime drinks while Teri was making Stephen's late-night feed. "And I can't help feeling glad that you've decided to get together again. It's better for a child that you should be living together again."

"It's only for a short time, Mother," Teri said warningly. "I could be back here within a couple of weeks."

"Oh, no, don't say that! I'm sure once you've been together for a while you'll both realise that you're happier together than apart," Bridget burbled romantically. "Now, I've made up the bed in the guest room. You can sleep in there."

"I shall sleep in my own room...with Stephen," said Teri stubbornly.

"But your bed is only a single one," twittered Bridget. "Damien can't possibly sleep with you in that."

"I don't care where Damien sleeps," retorted Teri, and picking up Stephen's bottle she went out of the room and up the stairs. She'd be glad to get to Skios, she thought. At least there no one would fuss about where she and Damien would sleep or whether they would sleep together or not. At least there, either in the house at Athens or in the villa on Skios, there were lots of rooms.

But twenty-four hours later, lying in the bedroom in the villa on Skios, looking at the stars swinging past the square of window, she went through the same torture she had gone through the first night she had stayed on that island, wondering where Damien was sleeping, wondering if he was with Melina.

As she might have expected, Tina took over the looking after of Stephen as if he were her own child, coming to him the next morning when he wakened, washing him, dressing him and then feeding him without bothering to ask Teri if she could.

"Don't be jealous," Damien mocked softly as they sat at breakfast when she complained that she had hardly seen the baby that morning. "Tina can probably look after him better than you can. After all, she looked after me from the time I was born and I didn't come to any harm."

"But that was different. Your mother had to go on working and perhaps she didn't want to look after you. I want to look after Stephen," Teri protested.

"Why?" he demanded abruptly.

"Why what?"

"Why do you want to look after him?"

"Because he's mine, of course."

"And mine," he retorted challengingly. "And now that he's here he's going to stay."

Teri set down the cup from which she had been sipping the thick sweet coffee. It was happening, what she had feared. Damien had tricked her into coming here with the baby and now he was going to take Stephen from her.

"You wouldn't be so cruel," she gasped through stiff lips. "You couldn't be so cruel as to take him from me!"

"I won't have to take him from you if you stay, will I?" he replied lightly, rising to his feet. "And now, if you'd like to go and get him we'll walk up to the other house to see my father."

She couldn't help feeling apprehensive as they walked along the path through the wind-twisted pines to the other villa. The day was sunny, but the wind off the sea was cool and high above in the blue arch of the sky puffy white clouds chased each other. The big villa looked the same, still possessed the same fairy-tale charm she remembered, its delicately carved pillars shimmering in the sunlight.

They went straight to the room which Stephanos

had always used and to Teri's surprise he was sitting in his wheelchair behind his **big** desk as if nothing had changed during the nine months or so since she had last seen him.

But she was shocked by the change in him. He seemed to have shrunk to half the size he had been before, seemed little more than a skeleton as he sat there watching her approach. Yet the fire was there in his eyes, leaping up to blaze when he saw Stephen.

"I'd like to hold him. Do you think I could hold him?" he said querulously, looking round at the square-shouldered, impassive woman in a nurse's uniform who stood by the wheelchair. He repeated the question in Greek and the woman answered him. It was then that Teri looked round the room for Melina. She wasn't there.

"Hand the baby to him." Damien's voice was quiet. "But stay near in case the strength goes from his hands suddenly."

She moved forward and kneeling down placed Stephen on Stephanos's knee. Thin claw-like hands curved around the tiny bundle. Stephanos muttered something in Greek and Teri saw tears slide down his emaciated cheeks. Then he looked up at her and his lips curved in a travesty of his old malicious grin.

"So you did it," he whispered. "You did it and survived."

"Yes, I did it," she replied, smiling at him.

"You chose well," he murmured, looking past her at Damien. "She has stamina and spirit, this girl. Treat her kindly and with respect and you'll never regret having married her." His glance came back to Teri. "Thank you for coming, my dear," he said. "Come again tomorrow. Come every day. You light up an old man's life."

They went from the room and lingered for a while

in one of the flower-bright, sun-warmed courtyards.

"What's the joke between you and Father?" Damien asked.

"He told me once he thought you might have made a mistake in choosing me to be your wife. He said I looked too narrow in the hips to be a good breeder of children. He was right—I am. I had to have a Caesarean."

"*Christo!*" The oath was ripped out savagely and his fingers bit into her arm as he swung her round to face him. Almost murderous in their fiery glare, his eyes searched her face. "Why wasn't I told? Why have you kept everything from me?"

Disturbed by the sound of his voice, Stephen, who was still in her arms, began to whimper.

"Damien, you're hurting my arm! Please, let go," Teri protested. "I...I...didn't tell you because I didn't think...I mean, I didn't want you to come and take the baby away from me," she muttered in a muddled way.

He let go of her arm abruptly, almost flinging it away from him, and began to go down the flight of stone steps which led from the courtyard to a lower level. He was waiting for her at the bottom, ready to guide her towards the path through the pines, and for a while they walked in silence. Then at last Damien spoke, his voice strangely hoarse and strained.

"Will you...if you were to have another baby would you have to have another operation?" he asked.

"Perhaps."

They walked on a little further down the hill. Through the branches of the trees Teri could see the glint of the sea. The sound of the water smashing against rocks carried upwards quite clearly.

"It doesn't matter," said Damien abruptly as if talking to himself.

"What doesn't matter?" she asked, and he stopped walking to turn to her. Sunlight filtered between the branches of the trees striped his face with golden light. Wearing casual clothes, a loose-fitting Greek shirt patterned in black, red and white, the slit opening revealing the hairs on his chest, and thigh-moulding, hip-hugging flared pants, his hair ruffled by the breeze, he was the man who had captivated her during their honeymoon, a vigorous pagan who delighted in all kinds of physical activity, and she felt desire uncoil itself low down in the pit of her stomach.

"It doesn't matter if you can't have any more children," he said slowly, and reaching out laid his hands on the bundle of clothes that was Stephen. "Let me carry him for a while," he added gently. "You look tired."

"No, I don't suppose it does matter," she said rather drearily, letting him take the baby from her. Now that his son had been born before Stephanos died it didn't matter any more if she didn't have any more children. He had achieved his purpose. And after Stephanos died he would be able to divorce her, perhaps marry Melina, who would be able to produce a dynasty, she was sure. "Melina wasn't there," she said as she followed him down the path, rubbing her right arm with her left hand, trying to ease the stiffness left from holding the baby.

"He sent her away," he said over his shoulder. "She was here when he came back from New York, but he told her to go away."

"Why?"

"I don't know. He didn't tell me," he replied, and strode ahead of her into the villa.

Well, at least that meant she wouldn't be tormented any more when she went to bed. She wouldn't be wondering if he was spending the night with Melina at the other villa, and she felt suddenly lighthearted, as if a great burden had been lifted from her.

The next few weeks had a strangely peaceful quality as Stephanos lingered on the brink of death, and Teri, caring for Stephen with Tina's help, didn't let herself look once beyond the moment when the old man would die. She went to visit him every day as he had requested. Sometimes Damien was with her, sometimes he wasn't, because he was in Athens at the head offices of the Nikerios organisation. When he was there she was glad of his company, and it seemed to her that slowly and cautiously each of them was learning a little more about the other as they explored through conversation each other's mind, always keeping away from the subjects which might cause them to quarrel.

Like their honeymoon, those two weeks were a time out of mind. Although there was no physical contact between them they were growing closer and closer to each other. If only it could go on forever, Teri found herself wishing. If only they could stay on this island and lead a life uninterrupted by outside problems.

But inevitably it came to an end. One night Stephanos's condition deteriorated rapidly and the next day the youngest of his daughters, Katina, arrived, bringing with her her daughters and also, much to Teri's surprise, Melina. Soon afterwards Andrea and her husband arrived from New York. Teri was glad that she didn't have to put them up. The big villa absorbed them easily and there were plenty of servants to wait on them there. But their coming meant she no longer had Damien to herself, and once again she began to worry about his relationship with Melina.

To her surprise Marilyn Wemsley, Damien's mother, arrived on Skios a few hours before Stephanos died. She had come, she said, because Stephanos had asked for her. Tall and elegant, beautifully dressed in a black woollen suit of classic simplicity, with thick dark hair and big golden eyes, she looked very much younger than she was.

"Also I wanted to meet you," she drawled, with just a hint of a nasal New York accent. "I'm not at all pleased with you and Damien, you know."

"Oh? Why not?" Teri bristled, ready to do battle.

"You've had that beautiful baby and made me a grandmother. Now everyone will guess my age," complained Marilyn, and sinking down gracefully onto the armchair in Teri's bedroom she raised her hands to her head and removed her hair, revealing that under the wig of black curls she had thin, greyish-black hair, cut very short. Across the room her bright eyes twinkled with amusement at Teri's surprised face. "There! I've paid you the greatest compliment I can—I've taken off my wig in your presence." Her glance raked Teri. "I can see why Damien fell for you. You're quite something. Now tell me all about poor old Stephanos."

During the next three days Teri was glad of Marilyn's presence on the island. With her humour and often outrageous comments she provided an antidote to the heavy, gloomy behaviour of the Nikerios clan, and after the funeral was over she sat with Teri in the room which would always be associated with Stephanos while the contents of his will were made available to the family.

"It's all so much Greek to you, I guess," said Marilyn in her humorous way.

"Do you understand it?" asked Teri.

"Oh, sure. My mother was Greek and taught me the language, and there was a time when I used to sing Greek songs à la Nana Mouskouri!" said Marilyn. "God, listen to them!" she exclaimed at Katina and Andrea burst into speech, seeming to be arguing volubly with the lawyers, with their husbands, with Damien, with one another. "Damien's ugly half-sister. Terrible, aren't they, quarrelling over the spoils. Let's go out, you and I, for a little walk. I'll be leaving soon. Damien has made arrangements for a helicopter to come and whisk me off to Athens, and there are a few things I want to talk to you about."

They walked slowly through the courtyard and down the stairs through the pines.

"They hate my guts, you know, those two. They hate me because I had Damien," Marilyn confided. "You've heard, I expect, how Stephanos and I came to be married?"

"I've heard a little. Paul told me," said Teri.

"Oh, him. I couldn't help thinking he was looking a little put out today when the will was being read. But then with the birth of Stephen, Andrea's dear little Paul lost his chances of inheriting a goodly portion of Stephanos's loot. You know who Stephanos's first wife was?"

"No, I don't think so," answered Teri, a little bewildered by her frank mother-in-law's strange remarks.

"She was Cassandra Voulgaris, only daughter of Georg Voulgaris, the shipping magnate for whom Stephanos used to work. Stephanos was her third husband and the only one who could make her pregnant. He married her because through her he knew he could one day take over control of the Voulgaris empire. And he did. It became the Nikerios empire. But Cassandra died in childbirth and their only son died with her, and for Stephanos the desire for a son became a sort of mania. That was why he married me when he heard that as the result of a brief affair we had once when he was visiting New York I had Damien. It was a business arrangement, and in return for a certain amount of money I let Stephanos have the custody of Damien when I divorced him a year later."

"Yes, I had heard that," Teri muttered.

"And you were shocked, of course."

"A little, but later...I think I understood."

"We weren't in love, you see, Stephanos and I, and I couldn't have stayed with him once I'd met those two ugly daughters of his. I couldn't stay where I was hated so much. They hate Damien too because Stephanos always preferred him to them, and now they hate you because you're married to him and have produced that darling little boy, causing Stephanos to change his will at the last minute."

"Change it?" echoed Teri. "How do you know he changed it?"

"Damien told me. That's why they were all quarrelling in there. That's why young Paul looked so sick." Marilyn turned to Teri as they reached the door to the room she had been using during her stay at the villa. "I've heard that you and he were very friendly when you first came out here. I think you're going to find he won't be quite so friendly now. Your son has come between him and the fortune he might have inherited as Stephanos's only grandson." Marilyn's tawny eyes narrowed thoughtfully. "He came between you and Damien, didn't he? It's because of him you left last year, isn't it?"

"I...no, it isn't. He and I were just friends. There was nothing serious between us," Teri protested. "But he did tell me why Damien married me. He did say it was because...." She broke off, remembering she was talking to her husband's mother and that Marilyn might not like to hear that her son was just as devious as his father had been.

"I knew it," sighed Marilyn. "He tried to cause trouble between you. He'd been put up to it by his mother, the jealous bitch that she is. What did he say about Damien? Come on, tell me! There isn't much you can say about my son that will shock me, you know."

"Paul said that...that Damien married me so that his father wouldn't guess he was having an affair with Melina," Teri said slowly.

"My God, that was clever!" exclaimed Marilyn. "She's one of them, you know. She's a cousin of theirs. They introduced her to Stephanos when he was ill, recommended her as a good nurse and then pushed her at Damien. They wouldn't have minded at all if she had his child because that would have kept it in the family, so to speak. And that's why Stephanos married her, conniving devil that he was. He didn't want Damien to marry into his first wife's family."

There was no more time for Marilyn to talk to her because Arnie appeared with the news that the helicopter had arrived. Before she went, however, Marilyn gave Teri a hug and an affectionate kiss.

"I'm glad my boy has found someone like you," she said. "Stay with him, Teri. He needs a lot of loving and he hasn't been lucky in the women he's known—including me, his mother."

The afternoon drifted into evening. Stephen was put to bed and Teri wandered up the path through the pines to the big villa in search of Damien, pondering on all that Marilyn had told her. Now that the funeral was over the time for her to face up to what she should do next was close. The time had come for her to leave Damien again. But she didn't want to leave him, not again, not ever. She wanted to stay with him because she loved him. The trouble was she couldn't be sure he loved her, perhaps would never be sure, because of the circumstances in which they had met and had married.

If only they could go back in time, meet again without that debt of her father's being between them, souring their relationship from the beginning, she was sure they would have fallen in love naturally. If only she hadn't listened to Paul! If only....

About to step into the wide lounge of the other villa, thinking she would find Damien and the rest of the Nikerios family still there, talking and arguing, Teri stopped. The room was only dimly lit, but she could see quite clearly that there were two people in it, Damien and Melina. They were standing as she had often seen them standing close together talking—at least Melina was talking rapidly, almost hysterically, and even while Teri hesitated the woman burst into sobs and flung herself at Damien.

As Teri watched his arms go round the woman she felt as if she was participating in some sort of nightmare. She wanted to shout, "No, no, don't do that! I don't want it to happen. I don't want to know about it."

But she didn't say anything. Instead she turned and ran quickly along the passage, out into the courtyard, and seeing an archway opening onto the darkness of the hillside she went through it.

CHAPTER SEVEN

DISTRESSED by what she had just seen, Teri didn't really notice where she was going until she realised she was walking uphill and not along the path which led down to Damien's villa. Coming to a stop, she looked round. Although the moon was up and could be seen, a round yellow disc gleaming in the eastern sky, patterned by the branches of shaggy windswept pines, it was difficult to make out her surroundings.

For a few moments she stood, listening to the wind sighing in the trees and looking down at the lights of the big villa, then beyond them to the lights of the other villa, close to the unseen shore. She couldn't go back yet. She couldn't go down there, and go to bed to lie there alone tormented with the thoughts that Damien was with Melina.

She turned, and looked upwards and saw the pillars of the small ruined temple etched against the moon-bleached sky. It would be better to walk up there than to lie sleepless and writhing with jealousy. Much better to be out here, under the stars and the moon. She would go up there, linger for a while and maybe find an answer to her problem.

Stones crunched under her feet and once or twice she almost walked into an outcrop of rock, but gradually her eyes became accustomed to the moon-light and she was able to make out the shapes of trees and the curve of the path. The temple was much higher up than she had thought and the path became very steep, developing into a series of high steps which led up to a plateau caught among cliffs of rock.

By the time she reached it she was breathless and the blood was racing along her veins, but she felt strangely elated when after negotiating the last steep slope she was able to stand up straight and look around, catching her breath in delight at the view of the moon, now silver, sailing along in the windy sky, dazzling the sea with its light.

Around her the pillars, the steps and pedestals, the old stone altars of the ancient sanctuary were bathed in silvery light while their shadows were deeply black, stretching across the remains of a mosaic floor, falling off the edge of it into the dark deeps of a ravine. Up there, the wind was stronger than below, whipping her hair into a tangle, lifting the edge of her skirt, seeming to push her towards the ravine.

Teri turned from the edge and shouted out loud when something flicked her cheek—a bat, zooming blindly about, disturbed by her presence. Far below she could see the twinkle of lights from the villas. They looked a long way down. The wind whined a little in rocky crevices and not too far away olive trees whispered sibilantly.

Finding a convenient slab of stone which had once been the support for a statue, perhaps, Teri sat down. Thousands of years ago people had brought offerings here, gifts to whatever god or goddess had presided over the temple. Sometimes their gifts had been made of gold or bronze, if they had been rich. Sometimes their gifts had been animal, a goat or a sheep, whatever they could spare if they had been poor. Whatever they brought as a sacrifice, they had all come with one thing in mind, to ask the god or goddess to intercede on their behalf.

Perhaps they had asked for health to be returned to a sick child or other member of their family. Perhaps some of them, women, had asked to be made fertile. Perhaps some of them, the young women or the young men, had asked for help in their amatory affairs and had prayed for their love for another to be requited.

Teri glanced round the moonlit circle towards the biggest block of stone of all, which had surely been the altar. She had no gift to offer except the gold chain around her neck or the wedding ring which was back on her finger. Her hand went to her throat, fingering the chain which had been Damien's gift. He had given her so many things since she had married him; clothing, jewellery, a house in Athens, a beautiful child. He had given her everything a woman could desire except the one thing she wanted: his love.

Her smile was a little twisted. Perhaps that was what she should ask for while she was here. Perhaps she should ask for Melina to be taken away and for Damien to love herself as she loved him. But what good would asking do? It wouldn't change the fact that she had seen Damien take Melina in his arms this evening. It wouldn't make her any less suspicious of him or trust him. The choice was hers and no ancient god once worshipped by an ancient people could help her. She could either stay and turn a blind eye to the fact that Melina existed and was Damien's mistress, no matter what his mother had said to the contrary. Or she could leave him again.

Her independent, freedom-loving spirit dictated that she should leave. She didn't have to stay and be humiliated. She would go, tomorrow, and she would take Stephen with her. She wasn't going to leave him behind to be hated by Melina as Damien had been hated by his half-sisters. She wasn't going to leave her child in the care of another woman. And if Damien wanted him, claimed custody of him according to the contract they had signed, she would fight him in court.

Feeling better for having made a decision, wondering with a touch of humour whether the ancient god or goddess had listened to her problem and had answered, Teri got to her feet, took one last look at the three silvery pillars shining against the sky and found her way to the edge of the floor where she thought she had climbed up.

Going down was much more difficult than coming up had been because the shadows thrown by the rocks were deceiving. Several times she lost her footing and slid down on her bottom, feeling sharp points of rock slice through her underwear and scratch her skin, and after one severe fall was so shaken that it was a long time before she could summon enough courage to continue on her way, she was so afraid she might step forward into space and go tumbling down the hillside non-stop, breaking her neck in the process and lying forever, hidden from view, until she died and birds came to eat her flesh and peck her eyes out.

But she did go on and at last came to more level ground, only to realise that she had lost all sense of direction, and not being able to see the twinkle of lights any more she did not know where the villas were. She was near a grove of olives, she knew that because she could hear the continuous whisper of their leaves. The moon must be situated in the south-east by now and the villas were both on the western side of the island, so if she turned her back on the moon and walked away from it she would find them...eventually.

She did find the beginning of a path leading down

through the olives. It twisted and turned a lot and when at last she came out of the trees she found she was facing the moon again. But she could see lights twinkling below her and that gave her hope, so she continued along the path, finding that it wound down the hillside in a series of broad zigzags following the lines of the terraces of vines and finally dropping down to a group of small cube-shaped houses huddled below the terraces, close to the moon-dazzled sea.

The first house she came to was a two-storeyed building. The lower storey opened right into a court-yard and seemed to be the place where the animals lived, judging by the strong mixture of goat and horse smells. Stone steps slanted up the outside wall to the other storey and light gleamed out from a window up there.

Teri went up the steps on to a wide stone platform, edged with walls where tubs of flowering shrubs stood and a vine of bougainvillea overhung a trellis made from the rough branches cut from pine trees. After a slight hesitation, during which time she dredged her memory for some Greek words, she knocked at the door.

It was opened by a woman, whose round dark eyes went even rounder with astonishment when she saw who had knocked. Teri said 'good evening' in Greek and then let out a sigh of exasperation as she realised she didn't know enough words to explain that she was lost.

The woman answered her politely enough, then raising her voice shouted raucously over her shoulder to someone within the house. In a few seconds a man loomed large against the light. He had a broad olive-skinned face and a grey moustache. It seemed to Teri that his eyes flashed with recognition when he saw her.

"You speak English, *kyrie*?" she asked, remembering some more of the Greek Paul had taught her, and to her relief he nodded. "I've been for a walk and I'm lost," she went on in English. "Could you please direct me to Kyrios Nikerios's villa?"

He gaped at her in surprise and said something to the woman in rapid Greek. The woman disappeared inside and the man swung the door open wider, making a welcoming gesture.

"Come in, come in, Kyria Nikerios," he said. "Come and wait while I get the carriage ready. Then I will drive you home."

"Oh, you're the man who drives one of the carriages," exclaimed Teri, suddenly recognising him.

"That is right, *kyria*," he said. "I am Patros Parara. This is my wife Irene, and my children Christos and Christina."

The room into which he led her was square and smelt of oil from the cooking of the supper. The walls were whitewashed and decorated with religious pictures painted in bright primitive colours. Over the scrubbed wooden table a single electric light bulb hung with its light shining on the silky black hair of the two children, one about twelve, the other about ten, who sat there, scooping up a mess of food from bowls. In one corner of the room was an old-fashioned oil cooker and above it were shelves for pans and dishes. Against another wall was a big bed covered with a rough grey blanket. On the wall over the bed was an icon of the Virgin Mary and Jesus. A small red light glowed before it. The room was very poor but spotlessly clean.

"Please sit down, *kyria*," Patros invited. "My wife will give you something to drink and eat while you wait."

"Thank you, thank you. You are very kind," said

Teri in her stumbling Greek, and the woman's sad, severe face was transformed temporarily by a smile which revealed her to be younger than Teri had at first thought. Patros went out and watched by two pairs of curious black eyes Teri sipped milk from the mug which had been placed before her. The milk smelt of goat and had a strong taste which made her stomach heave, but she drank most of it, realising that she was hungry having by now missed supper. The dish of food which she was offered also smelt strongly, this time of fish. It seemed to be a mixture of bits of some sort of fish, onions, rice currants and pine nut kernels and actually tasted delicious. Teri ate it all, feeling guilty because the house was so poor compared with the houses she had lived in while she had been in Greece.

By the time she had finished eating, Patros was back, and after thanking Irene again Teri followed him down the steps to the yard where the carriage in which she had ridden with Damien and later with Paul, from the port to the villas, was waiting.

It was a beautiful night for riding along the coast road with the moon silvering the sea and the little waves sparkling as they tumbled on to the shore. Leaning back in the carriage seat, Teri let her mind drift back to the first time she had ridden with Damien and he had put an arm around her and had kissed her. She wished suddenly that he was with her now, to touch her knee suggestively, to gather her in his arms, to force her lips apart with his. The longing for him to make love to her shuddered through her, titillating tiny nerves which had long been dormant, causing her head to reel with sensuousness. Alarmed by the effect just thinking about Damien making love to her had had on her, she stiffened and sat up straight for the rest of the ride.

At last the lights of Damien's villa came into view. Every light seemed to be on. The whole place was ablaze with them and as the carriage came to a stop in the lower courtyard she heard Arnie's voice shouting something. The main door was wide open and Damien appeared in the opening, a dark figure against the brightness of the light before he seemed to hurry forward and stride up to the carriage, his hand reaching up to help her down.

"Where have you been?" he demanded roughly, his hands gripping her arms bruisingly. "Where in the name of God have you been?" By the light shafting out of the house she could see his face was quite haggard and that his eyes seemed to be on fire.

"I went for a walk...up to the temple," she said.

"In the dark?" he exclaimed incredulously. "You could have mistaken your way, fallen down the ravine. *Christo*," the oath hissed savagely, his breath flicking her cheek like a whip, "have you no sense? No sense at all?" He was shaking her wildly.

"No, I haven't," she spat at him, wrenching herself free from his bruising hands. "Oh, pay him!" she cried. "Please, Pay Mr. Parara for bringing me home. Give him lots and lots of money. They're so poor. You wouldn't believe how poor their home is, and yet they gave me food and drink." She turned to the carriage driver, said thank you again and rushing past the amazed-looking Arnie and Tina, who had come out into the courtyard to see what was going on, she ran into the house round the main part of the house and up the steps to the room where she slept.

Once there, aghast at the sight of her wild appearance in the mirror, she went straight into the bathroom. She lingered a long time in the bath examining the various bruises and scratches she had sustained during her walk. When at last she stepped out of the water she felt soothed and calm and knew exactly how she was going to deal with Damien. Since she hadn't brought any night clothes with her into the bathroom, after she had dried herself she wound the biggest towel about her sarong-wise and went through into the bedroom, pulling up short when she saw that Damien was lying on the bed, head and shoulders propped against the pillows. As soon as he saw her he swung off the bed and with his hands in the pockets of his black velour dressing gown which was all he seemed to be wearing, judging by his bare legs, bare feet and bared chest, he came towards her.

"Are you all right?" he asked. There was no fire in his eyes now as their glance ranged over her. Shadowed by their long lashes and by his frowning brows, they were as black and fathomless as the ravine had been near the temple.

"Yes, of course I'm all right," she answered, stepping past him and going over to a chest of drawers to select a clean nightgown.

"You were so long in there that I was beginning to wonder if you'd fainted...or drowned," he told her, coming after her and speaking behind her right shoulder. She knew he was standing just there because she felt his breath waft her bare skin. At one time he would have come into the bathroom without knocking to see her in the bath, perhaps even to join her in it...Teri bit her lip, took hold on her flighty thoughts and concentrated on finding the right nightgown. Taking it out of the drawer, she slipped it over her head without turning round. Her arms sought the armholes and she felt the gown being lifted as Damien helped her put it on. Once her arms were through the holes the gown swirled about her in a haze of sea-green chiffon nylon. With one tug she had the towel off and let it drop to the floor. Bending, she picked it up, side-stepped past Damien again and going back into the bathroom she hung the towel on a rail, collected up her discarded clothing and pushed everything into the dirty-clothes basket and then after switching off the bathroom door light she went back into the bedroom.

"Why did you go up to the temple?" Damien asked.

"I had some thinking to do," she replied, going across to the dressing table and sitting down on the stool. Picking up her hairbrush, she began to brush her hair, watching her own reflection—white arms lifted up, white-gold hair glittering like tangled Christmas tinsel in the electric light, her face pale as marble, red lips set in a stubborn wilful line, dark blue eyes wary and watchful.

He came up behind her again to stand behind her, a dark sinister shadow in his black robe, accentuating her fairness. As the brush lifted from her hair he caught hold of her hand and after a token resistance she let him take the brush from it. Slowly, with strong strokes, he began to brush her hair, his head bent so that all Teri could see properly was his broad brow and the black hair curving down on to it.

She drew a deep breath, clutched at the edge of the stool with both hands and said in a clear steady voice,

"Damien, I'm going back to London tomorrow and I'm taking Stephen."

In the mirror she watched the brush complete a stroke, start another and complete that, then start another. Without speaking Damien went on brushing her hair until all the tangles were out of it and it coiled in its usual wiry ringlets down to her shoulders. The brushing done apparently to his satisfaction he tossed the brush on to the dressing table and rested his hands lightly on her shoulders, looked directly at her reflection, his eyes meeting hers, a faint smile softening the line of his mouth.

"Now you look more like the woman I married," he murmured. "Wayward, a little spoilt."

In a sort of fascination she watched his hands slide forward and downwards over her breasts, fingers probing familiarly through the thin silky material of her nightgown. As she felt dangerously sensual tingles dance along her nerves she leaned forward, hoping to free herself from that suggestive embrace, but his hands merely slipped further downward to her waist and she was pulled back against him.

"Damien, didn't you hear what I said?" she demanded, trying to make her voice sound cold and cutting, but to her annoyance it shook.

"Yes, I heard," he said softly. "But I didn't like what I heard." In the mirror she saw light shining on the silky texture of his hair as he bent his head. She felt that silkiness brush against her skin, then the burning heat of his lips in the curve of her neck. "Come to bed," he whispered, raising his head and looking at her from just over her shoulder. "I want you and you want me."

"No, I don't. I don't!" she cried, her hands on his trying to lift them away from her body.

"Yes, you do. You think I can't feel your heart racing as mine is!" he murmured, the fingers of his left hand spreading upwards over her breast, seeking and finding the tender point. Teri gasped, and her body arched backwards involuntarily, her lips parted and her eyelids drooped. "You see?" mocked the voice of her tormentor, and then his arms closed around her, lifting her to her feet. Still she tried to escape, but he kicked aside the stool which was between them, caught her up against him and carrying her walked towards the bed.

"Damien, you promised you wouldn't take any advantage if I came here," she hissed, kicking with her legs and trying to writhe her way out of his arms.

"Did I? Then I am breaking that promise right now," he retorted. "I can't help it, forgive me Teri, but I can't help it. You're so beautiful, my wayward, angelic-looking wife and it's been so long...too long...."

With one leg across both of hers, he loomed over her where she lay on the bed, one hand caressing her throat, while his dark eyes seemed to feast on her face. Slowly his face came down closer to hers as his hand slid down to probe her breast again suggestively.

"Can you honestly say you don't want me now?" he whispered, his lips hovering tantalisingly above hers, and as the flames of passion ignited by his seductive fingers scorched through her she gave a little moan of surrender and lifting her hands to his face drew it closer until their lips met.

From then on nothing else mattered except the satisfaction of their desperate need for each other. It seemed that both of them had been starved of kisses and caresses during the past seven months and now couldn't get enough of them. Nor, so it seemed, could they get enough of touching each other, sighing with delight when an old familiar sensation was aroused, gasping in an agony of pleasure when a new one was triggered off by caressing fingertips, biting teeth or by the close entwining of limbs.

It was long and it was joyous, that worshipping of each other's body and their coming together was violent but ecstatic, a realisation and yet a satisfaction too of all their desires, and when it was over they lay for a long time, black hair entangled with blond, arms and legs entwined, not speaking to each other because there was after all no need for words, until they both fell asleep.

Teri slept heavily as if drugged, waking only when she heard the sound of the bedroom door opening. Turning her head on the pillow, surprised to find she was naked under the bed coverings, she watched Tina enter the room with a tray. The whole scene was familiar to her. It had been played several times since she had met Damien, this waking to find herself alone in a bed where they had found such pleasure in each other and to see either Tina or another housekeeper entering the room with a breakfast tray.

The room was dim, but she could tell it was full daylight because bright shafts of sunshine were slanting into the room between the slats of the shutters covering the window.

"What time is it?" she asked, stretching lazily beneath the covers, luxuriating in the delicious lassitude which lapped her whole body, smiling a little to herself as she recalled how it had been attained. Oh, she and Damien made love together very well and she doubted very much if she would ever find anywhere another lover who could satisfy her the way he could. She didn't want to find one, either.

"Noon," said Tina impassively. Having set down the tray she stood by the bed, hands folded in front of her on her white apron, that old hostile glint in her dark eyes.

"What?" Teri sat up in the bed, remembered her nakedness too late and clutched the sheet to her breasts to cover them as she stared disbelievingly at the other woman. "Why didn't you wake me before?'' she demanded, her glance going to the other pillow which was all crushed and dented. Why hadn't Damien wakened her, she wondered dismally. Why did he never wake her? Why did he always leave her while she slept, as if, like a thief in the night, having taken what he wanted, he had to be gone before daylight?

"Kyrios Nikerios said I was to let you sleep as long as possible. He said you were very tired and needed a long rest," replied Tina coolly.

"But what about the baby?" Teri exclaimed, realising that this was the first time in seven weeks she had not been wakened by Stephen crying to be fed.

"When he woke this morning Kyrios Nikerios attended to him and brought him to the kitchen to be fed. Now the baby is asleep in the courtyard. He is quite happy to be looked after by his father and by me," said Tina, implying no doubt that the child did not need herself, thought Teri wryly. "You have your breakfast now, *kyria*," Tina added, nodding towards the tray. "The helicopter is back from Athens and will convey you and the child there, when you are ready to go."

"Oh." Teri frowned as she digested this piece of information. "Do I have to go to Athens?" she asked.

"Kyrios Nikerios said you do. He said you are going to England maybe tomorrow, because it is too late for you to go today. He has already gone to Athens and asked me to tell you he will make reservations for you on a flight to London tomorrow. He will see you at the house in Athens later this afternoon."

Tina gave her another inimical glare and turning, went out of the room. As soon as the door had closed Teri leapt from the bed and ran across to the closet, dragged her dressing gown from its hanger and wrapped it around her. Going back to the bedside table, she gulped down the thick coffee, shuddering a little at its sweetness, then spread butter and honey on a chunk of bread. She ate ravenously, and all the time her thoughts were skittering in every direction as she tried to guess what the unpredictable Damien was up to now.

It was very obliging of him to make reservations on the flight to London for her, she thought with a wry twist of her lips, especially after what had happened last night. One might almost believe he hadn't meant a word he had said last night about wanting her, about finding her a more beautiful and a more satisfactory lover than any other woman he had known, about being glad she was his wife and the mother of his son.

She sat down suddenly on the bed, her hands clutching at the tumbled sheets as she fought to keep back threatening tears. What was the matter with her? Where was her spirit, her pride? Was she always going to let herself be hurt by a man who cared so little about her that he often left her bed before she woke up, treating her as if she were no more than a mistress, a woman he had paid to sleep with?

But there had been times during the past weeks, while they had lived here together, when she had had the impression that Damien did care for her, and even now she could feel the bruising pressure of his fingers on her arms last evening when he had helped her down from the carriage. He had been upset because she had been missing, furiously angry with her because she had gone walking in the dark and might have fallen down a precipice.

"Are you ready, *kyria*?" Tina was back, peeping round the edge of the door. "Shall I lift the baby and prepare him for the journey in the helicopter?"

"No, not yet. I have to pack—everything. You see, I won't be coming back," said Teri wildly.

Tina helped her pack and Tina got Stephen ready for the journey, laying him in his carrycot which she carried herself and delivered to the pilot of the helicopter as if she didn't trust Teri to do the right thing. Flying in a helicopter wasn't a new experience for Teri because she had come from Athens in this one three weeks previously, but the take-off still made her catch her breath.

This could be the last time she saw Skios, she thought as she watched the tiny harbour slide by beneath her. It might be the last time she saw the sea in which the tiny island was set among other islands, the islands of Greece, created, so the story was told, after God had created the rest of the earth. Finding He had a handful of rocks left over He had scooped them up, tossed them over His mighty shoulder and they had become the islands of Greece.

Jade green, turquoise and purple were the colours of the sea and the islands were blobs of ochre-coloured rock and shimmering olive green. And in the distance the mountains of the mainland glittered silver and gold against the cloud-streaked blue sky.

Across the Saronic Gulf the helicopter swooped towards Athens airport, whirling down towards the pad with a clatter. Teri had wild thoughts of finding her way to the terminal buildings and an airline desk and of trying to get on a plane which would take her at least part way to England that evening, but as soon as she realised Stephen had already been taken in his carrycot by the pilot of the helicopter in the direction of the Nikerios Cadillac which was parked conveniently near the landing place, she hurried after him.

The chauffeur of the car greeted her with grave politeness and within a few minutes the airport was being left behind as the car sped smoothly along the wide highway towards Athens. It was with a feeling of having come home that Teri recognised places and streets and as always glimpses of the Acropolis, appearing suddenly and dramatically as the car turned corners, its marble pillars glowing in the light of the westering sun, seeming to shame the clusters of highrise apartment buildings which were trying to hide it from her view, gave her the usual thrill of excitement.

Another emotion, a strangely satisfied glow of possessiveness, coursed through her when at last the car turned in through the gates of the small villa on the slopes of Mount Lykavitos, and she could not help feeling glad that it was here, at her house, her very own house, that Damien intended to meet her this afternoon and not at the big, empty echoing mausoleum of the Nikerios villa.

No one came to the front door to greet her, however, and she stood before it uncertainly, wondering if she had her key with her. The chauffeur came up the steps with Stephen's carrycot and set it down, and to her surprise took a key from his pocket. He inserted it in the lock, turned it and then pushed open the door, indicating that she should enter before him.

The air of the house was warm and slightly fusty as if the place had been closed up for some time, yet there was no sign of dust on the furniture. No sign of the place having been lived in recently either, Teri thought as she wandered into the lounge and looked around and wondered what had happened to Anika and the other servants who had looked after the house during the short time she had lived in it.

Hearing the front door close, she hurried back into the hall. Her two suitcases and the small zipped bag in which she carried Stephen's things were standing just inside the door and Stephen was crying lustily, his little legs kicking off the covers in the carrycot, which was also on the floor. But the chauffeur had gone and even as Teri went towards the door to open it and run out to him to ask him if he knew when Damien would be coming, she heard the engine of the car start up, followed by the sound of the vehicle moving away.

Stephen's protests could be ignored no longer, so she carried him into the living room and began to change him. When that was done she went on an exploration of the house, carrying him with her on her hip. The kitchen was clean, its equipment still very new-looking and hardly used, and the cupboards and refrigerator were loaded with food. Upstairs the bed in her bedroom was made up with clean sheets and in the small dressing room off it there was a very new-looking baby's cot, complete with sheets and blankets.

Puzzled by the signs that there had been someone in the house that day and by the fact that there was no one there now, Teri went back downstairs and taking the carrycot with her went into the kitchen. There, for the next hour, with Stephen in the carrycot and able to watch her as he kicked and gurgled, she prepared some food for herself and made up the milk for his next feed.

She expected Damien to come before Stephen's bedtime, but the baby was already fast asleep, the sun had long set and she was at the window of the living room looking out at the glittering city lights, her nerves strung taut with waiting, when she heard the familiar roar of a sports car's exhaust coming up the drive.

It was with great difficulty that she controlled an urge to rush out into the hallway and fling open the

front door in welcome. She waited until the front door
had opened and closed before she advanced to the
archway of the living room entrance.

"I thought you would be here sooner," she said.
Damien dropped the briefcase and suitcase he was carrying, raked a hand through his hair, tousling it, and
came towards her, one hand at the knot of his tie loosening it, disbelief expressed plainly in his eyes as they
met hers, an expression which gave way quickly to
one of wariness.

"It's been one hell of a day," he told her. "So
many problems to solve, so many people to see now
that my father...." He rubbed a hand wearily across
his forehead and stepped past her into the room. "Is
Stephen asleep?" he asked.

"Yes."

"You found everything all right?" he asked, swinging round to face her as she followed him. "The cot
and...."

"Yes, yes," she interrupted him. "But where is
everyone? There was no one here when I came.
Where are Anika and the others?"

"They haven't been here since you left last year. I
closed the house up," he replied, turning away from
her again and going across to a cabinet where glasses
and liquor were stored. "It's good to be here, where
it's quiet," he muttered half to himself. "At the other
house, those two bats out of hell, Andrea and Katina,
were squabbling all day over who should have what,
and before that I had Melina to cope with...."

"Melina?" she repeated, watching him open a
bottle of *ouzo* and pour some of the liquor into a
glass.

"That's right. He made no provision for her, you
know. Left her completely out of his will. I had to do

something to help her. That's why I came over here
with her early this morning." He drank all that was in
the glass and set it down.

"Did you remember to make the reservation on
the flight to London tomorrow, for me and
Stephen?" she asked. "Tina told me you were going
to."

"No, I didn't." He came across to her and from
under frowning eyebrows his eyes searched her face.

"Why not?" she demanded.

"I...." He broke off, frowning even more blackly,
and caught his lower lip with the edge of straight white
teeth. For the first time since she had met him Teri
thought he looked disconcerted. "I thought," he went
on slowly, his glance avoiding hers, "that after last
night, you might change your mind and stay...for a
while."

"Last night?" she queried lightly, with a shrug of
one shoulder, turning away from him now and stroll-
ing over to an armchair to perch on its arm. "What
was so special about last night?" she drawled, and
waited tensely for his anger to explode, examining
her nails because she didn't dare look at him. "It
didn't mean anything. It has never meant anything to
you. You're interested only in the physical side of
our relationship." She paused, drew a deep breath
and added shakily, "It's still you and Melina. You
still put her before me. You left me this morning to
bring her here. You...you treat her as if she's your
wife and you treat me as if I'm your mistress,
instead...instead of the other way round!"

Instead of his anger exploding it seemed as if silence exploded between them. It was a frightening,
electrifying silence in which Teri could hear her heart
pounding jerkily. Then she heard Damien move. The

pad of his feet on the thick pile of the carpet was stealthy, almost predatory.

"Would you mind explaining all that?" he said quietly. "You have confused me. What do you mean by saying it's still me and Melina?"

"You...she...you're in love with each other," she muttered. "You...you wish you were married to each other." She raised her head and glared at him defiantly. "Oh, don't deny it. I saw her in your arms last night...at your father's villa and...."

"So it was you I heard running away," he put in.

"You...you heard me?" she quavered.

"Yes. I went after you, called to you, but when I reached the courtyard you'd gone. I thought you must have gone back to our villa and so I went there too. But you weren't there and after waiting for you to turn up I began to think... *Christo!*" The oath hissed savagely. "Don't ever do that to me again, Teri! Don't ever go away from me without telling me where you're going," he muttered in a low fierce voice, and his hands came out to clutch either side of her head to hold her face lifted up to his as he bent to look deeply into her eyes. "Do you hear me?" he added softly, yet threateningly.

"Yes, I do," she whispered in reply, her hands going up to his wrists and closing round them. "But...but... you still have to explain about Melina."

"She was very upset because Poppa had left her out of his will and she had realised that both he and I had seen through Andrea's and Katina's little plots to turn him against me. I felt sorry for her and was trying to comfort her...."

"Oh yes, comforting her," she jibed, pulling his hands away from her head, letting go of them and sliding to her feet to wander away over to the window.

"You comforted me once, and look what happened," she added bitterly. "Or perhaps you've forgotten that."

"No, I haven't forgotten. You were very sweet and soft to hold and I couldn't help myself...." Damien broke off to swear again and Teri heard him come up behind her. His hands weren't gentle when they touched her shoulders, and he didn't give her a chance to free herself but dragged her against him and with his fingers under her chin forced her head back against his shoulder so that he could swoop in and plunder her mouth.

She came up sighing and limp from the depths of sensuousness into which that desperate, hungry kiss of his had plunged her. Groaning, Damien let go of her suddenly so that, still off balance, she staggered and would have fallen back against the window if he hadn't reached out again and hauled her back into his arms.

"You see, I can't help myself now," he whispered close to her ear. "Whenever I'm near you I have to touch you, make sure you're real. I have to get your attention somehow, make you want to touch me, be aware of me. You were right, just now, when you said I was more interested in the physical side of our relationship than any other part of it. I was. As soon as I set eyes on you in that gambling club in London I fell in love with you and wanted you. But there must have been, even then, something more than lust in the way I felt or I wouldn't have wanted to marry you. I wouldn't have felt jealous when I found out how you had been carrying on with Paul while I was in New York...."

"I didn't carry on with him," she protested, pushing away from him.

"Melina said you did."

"She saw us kiss...once...or twice."

"Once was more than enough," he growled. "It was Paul who made up stories about me and Melina for your benefit," he went on, still holding on to her arms. "And you believed him."

"It wasn't hard to believe. I could see with my own eyes how you and she got together and whispered secretly in corners. And then...then...the first night we were on Skios...our...our wedding night, you stayed half the night at your father's villa with her."

"I did not stay with her," he grated savagely. "I was with my father."

"Then why didn't you tell me?"

"I seem to remember you weren't very interested when at last I joined you. You were tired, you said," he whispered tauntingly, and she cried out as his sharp teeth nipped the lobe of her ear.

"And then after our honeymoon you didn't live with me properly in this house. You came and went...like...like a visitor," she retorted shakily, her hand sliding up over his chest, fingers groping between the buttons of his shirt.

"I thought it was what you wanted," he muttered, his voice muffled as he rubbed his cheek against her hair. "I knew you had married me for money, that for you it was a marriage of convenience and nothing else. You'd made that very clear from the outset and because...because I wanted you so much I went along with it, always hoping that one day you would learn to love me as I was learning to love you." His arms tightened around her. "Then you went away, left me without a word of explanation. Why did you walk out on me last year? Are you going to tell me now? I think I have a right to know."

"I told you in the note I left," she said.

"You told me nothing, called me names, that's all."

"I . . . well, surely you could guess from that why I'd left? You must have realised I'd found out . . . I mean, I . . . ." She paused, then muttered brokenly, hiding her face against his warm pulsing throat, "Oh, I believed what Paul told me about you. I believed you'd only married me because . . . you wanted to throw dust in your father's eyes and to . . . to . . . prevent him from cutting you out of his will by . . . by . . . producing an heir. And I couldn't bear it, I couldn't bear knowing that you were like that." Her hands crept up around his neck, her fingers tangling in the vigorous hair which curled at his nape, and she lifted her face to him appealingly. "You see, I . . . I was learning to love you," she whispered. "Only I didn't know it, I didn't recognise that I did until . . . until I realised I couldn't possibly get rid of your child."

"*Theos*, you considered doing *that*?" With his hands on her shoulders he pushed her away from him to stare at her with horrified eyes and she nodded dumbly, waiting for his anger to crash about her, but instead he drew her against him again, his arms enfolding her comfortingly. "You little fool," he whispered tautly. "You silly, wayward fool! Why would you want to do something like that? Why?"

"I . . . I . . . wanted to hurt you in some way, I suppose . . . because you . . . because I thought you didn't love me."

"I loved you. I love you now," he said fiercely, tilting her face to his and beginning to kiss it, the tender warmth of his lips touching her cheeks, her eyes, the tip of her nose. "And I want to show you that I do, like I did last night, but now I'm afraid to.

Oh, God, Teri...last night...I went out of my mind a little when you weren't at the villa and you didn't return. I thought perhaps you'd left me again and I wouldn't know where to find you, so that when you came back, I....I couldn't help myself." Again his voice became muffled as he buried his mouth in her hair. "Can you forgive me for what happened? I didn't take any precautions and I'm not sure if you did either. You...you could conceive again."

Understanding flooded Teri's mind with bright lights. He did care about her. There was much yet which had to be explained, but that could be done anytime, later tonight, or tomorrow, or the day after that, any time in the future months or years they were going to be together. Right now what mattered was that she should show him that she cared about him, enough to comfort him when he was distressed as he had comforted her, enough to share Stephen with him, enough to risk having another child by him.

"It's all right," she said softly and comfortingly, stroking the back of his head. "I'll be happy to have another child now I know how you feel and...and... the doctor didn't say I shouldn't have any more. In fact he said it might be easier for me...the second time."

Damien raised his head and looked down at her, his eyes dark and anxious, and she realised he was going to need a lot of convincing.

"You're sure?" he asked intently.

"I'm sure." Teri smiled up at him provocatively, her eyes glinting through the downward sweep of her lashes. "And if you need convincing, why not come visiting to my room tonight? After we've had supper, of course. I'll go and cook it now."

She slipped out of his arms and began to go towards the door, but he soon caught up with her, sliding an arm about her waist as they went out into the hallway.

"Can you cook?" he challenged.

"Of course I can."

"Greek food?"

"Well...I'll try."

In the end she had to have his help, but it was fun preparing the meal together, a shared happening, something which had been missing from their relationship before because there had always been other people around them, she realised.

"Do you realise this is the first time we've been in this house on our own?" she said as they sat eating by candlelight.

"It's the first time we have been in any house on our own," he replied. "Makes a difference, doesn't it? There's no one to distract our attention from one another, no one to interfere. That is why I hoped you would come today and why I told Anika you wouldn't be requiring her services, at least for a few days."

"You *hoped* I would come?" she repeated, watching him pour more wine into their glasses. "You didn't expect me?"

"I never expect you to do anything I ask," he retorted dryly. "You have always been very unpredictable."

"No more than you are," she shot back at him, but he only laughed at her.

"Do you still want to go back to London?" he asked.

"Not...not immediately," Teri replied cautiously, puzzled by the question. "Do...do...do you want me to go?"

"Not immediately," he mocked her with a wicked grin. Then he frowned in a puzzled way as he picked up his wine glass. "I'm still not clear as to why you left the last time. Would you mind telling me again what it was Paul told you about throwing dust in my father's eyes? Why would my marriage to you do that?"

Once again she told him all that Paul had told her. This time by answering his searching questions she was able to explain it more carefully, but by the time she had finished Damien was laughing helplessly.

"Damien!" she said sharply. "It wasn't funny at the time. Paul was extremely plausible and I had no difficulty in believing that you and your father had quarrelled. He was a very strong-willed man. And you are stubborn, you've told me so yourself."

"I know, I know." He wiped tears from his cheeks and sipped some wine. "It's true we did sometimes quarrel, but on the whole our relationship was amicable. He liked to tease me and did so often enough about my unmarried status. And that is what Paul probably overheard. The part about Poppa threatening to cut me out of his will if I didn't oblige him by getting married and producing an heir he made up, to suit his own ends."

"And they were?"

"To turn you against me so that you would leave me." Damien's glance was cold. "It worked, too, his little trick, didn't it? Instead of telling me what he told you, instead of giving me a chance to present another side to the picture, you went off in a huff."

"And I suppose it was just coincidence that you married me so soon after Paul overheard what he did," she countered sharply.

"It was, yes. Marriage was as far from my mind as it had ever been when I went to London, to settle that business of your father's debt." His mouth took on a wry curve. "I wasn't going to insist on it being paid, you know. Arranging security in that way was Alex's idea, not mine. He wouldn't accept help without us signing that agreement. My intention was to tear the agreement up, and to forget it... until I met you. Paul lied to you, Teri. I married you for only one reason, because I had fallen in love with you."

"Then...then...why did you let me leave you?" she protested. "Why didn't you follow me to England?"

"You asked me not to," he exclaimed, his eyes widening. "You said you didn't want to see me again." His mouth curved even more bitterly. "I have some pride too, you know. And it was hard to take after all I had done to show you I loved you and cared about you. For quite a while after you'd gone I thought—what the hell, you were no better and no worse than any other woman I'd known, nothing more than a hard-faced bitch out for as much money as she could get settled on her in return for as little as she could give."

The harshness of his words made her flinch. He had come so close to describing the sort of person she had tried to be.

"I thought I could do it," she muttered. "I thought I could take and not give. I tried to. I tried hard not to love you, but all the time I was in Scotland I kept hoping you'd ignore what I had put in that note and come to see me."

"And I kept hoping you would write asking me to come," Damien replied. "But as the months went by and nothing happened I began to think up ways to see you without waiting for you to ask me. I looked around for excuses to approach you. My father's illness provided me with one which I thought might appeal to you."

"Didn't he ask to see me, then?" Teri exclaimed suspiciously.

"Many times." He paused and again the curve of his mouth was cynical. "I never told him you had left me, you know. I didn't want to admit failure, I suppose. I pretended you'd had to go to England on family business and would come back. Then I had to fight my pride. I found it hard to sink it and come after you. You see once, years ago, I fell in love with a woman who didn't return my love and I'd always vowed I would never let it happen again. Since then I'd always been the one who walked out of any relationship."

"Who was she?" asked Teri.

"Helga Sweiss, the archaeologist's wife."

"Then it was you who caused the scandal!" she exclaimed, remembering Paul's reference to something which had happened years ago on Skios about which the Nikerios family would never talk.

"It was me," Damien remarked. "I nearly eloped with her."

"Eloped? Why?"

"A good question," he mocked. "Why? She was beautiful, blond." His glance rested on her hair. "Different from you, more golden. And I was young, mostly Greek, hot-blooded, full of conceit and more than a little cocky when a mature, voluptuous woman, as Helga was then, responded to my inexpert but vigorous love-making. We had an affair, right there on the island, under the noses of the family. I guess I was sorry for her, too. She used to tell me about Carl, about how frigid he was and how he never made love to her." He picked up his wine glass and emptied it. "Are you sure you want to hear any more of the sordid details?" he asked dryly.

"Well, I'm not going to let you stop just there. What happened?"

"I had it all planned for us to run away together, to Italy. I was going to give her a house to live in." His mouth quirked again in self-mocking humour. "Oh, I had big ideas, I was so infatuated with her. And then Alex came to Skios to see Carl."

"So?"

Across the table his dark eyes assessed her, their glance lingered lovingly on her eyes and then her mouth.

"She lost interest in me and turned all her considerable charm on him."

"Oh, no!" Teri gasped, amazed by this new view of her father. "He didn't...they didn't...." she stammered.

"I don't know whether they did or they didn't, but I was so jealous, and my pride in myself was so offended because she seemed to prefer him to me, that one night I challenged him about it." This time the smile which curved his mouth was one of affectionate reminiscence. "He was very amused by me, I remember, but he calmed me down, soothed my ruffled feathers, I suppose, and he told me to beware of Helga, and women like her. He said she was only interested in me because I was the heir to millions and that once she had got what she wanted from me, she would probably walk out. He left the next day, and sure enough Helga turned her attentions to me again."

"What did you do?" Teri asked.

"Took Alex's advice," he replied quietly. "I found suddenly that I had a great interest in my father's shipping business, wanted to learn about it in the way he had done, from the deck of a freighter. I went to him and in a few days I was on an old tanker, bound for the Persian Gulf.''

''And Helga? What happened to her?''

''I don't know. I never saw her or Carl again. By the time I returned to Skios they had long been gone.'' He smiled at her. ''Now you know why I was so grateful to Alex and why I had to help him when he was in a financial mess? And I've just realised that if I hadn't lent it to him I would never have met you.''

''If you hadn't lent it to him I might not have been so distrustful of you and I'd never have believed what Paul said about you,'' she argued. ''Oh, what fools we've both been, letting pride come between us and letting other people form our opinions of each other. I'm so glad you came to Scotland and asked me to come and see your father.''

''Supposing I hadn't come for you, would you have come to me? Would you have told me about Stephen?'' he asked, and she sensed a certain reserve in his attitude.

''I think so,'' she whispered uncertainly. ''I...I... hadn't really decided what I was going to do once I'd left Scotland. Oh, please, Damien, don't look like that! Don't be hurt too much. I...I've never been able to plan any further than a day at a time ever since David was killed. Since then I've tried not to expect too much from life or from people. I've tried not to dream hopefully in case...in case things didn't work out the way I hoped they would.'' It was her turn to reach out and touch his hand. ''Please try to forgive me for not telling you about Stephen. I was so afraid that once you knew you would take him from me. But...but if I had written to you and had asked you to come and see me and him, would you have come?''

"I'd have come," he said simply, turning his hand to upcurl his fingers about hers and raise them to his lips.

"Then it's all right, isn't it?" she said. "I mean, if you'd have come we'd have found out like we've found out now how we feel, wouldn't we? It doesn't really matter how or why we got together again, does it? All that matters is that we did."

"That's all that matters," Damien agreed, rising to his feet and lifting her to hers. With an arm about her waist he began to lead her towards the door of the kitchen and into the hallway. "All that matters is that you're here and you're going to stay and supper is over. Now what was that you were saying about me visiting you in your bedroom later? I don't wish to seem too domineering or too insistent about claiming my marital rights, but I was thinking of moving into that room and taking up permanent residence there. Do you agree to that?"

"I agree," Teri replied happily, and together they walked slowly up the stairs.

Here's how to get your volume NOW!

MAIL IN	$	GET
2 SPECIAL PROOF-OF-PURCHASE SEALS*	PLUS $1 U.S.	ONE BOOK
5 SPECIAL PROOF-OF-PURCHASE SEALS*	PLUS 50¢ U.S.	ONE BOOK
8 SPECIAL PROOF-OF-PURCHASE SEALS*	FREE	ONE BOOK

*Special proof-of-purchase seal from inside back cover of all specially marked
Harlequin "Let Your Imagination Fly Sweepstakes" volumes.
No other proof-of-purchase accepted.

ORDERING DETAILS:

Print your name, address, city, state or province, zip or postal code on the coupon below or a plain 3" x 5" piece of paper and together with the special proof-of-purchase seals and check or money order (no stamps or cash please) as indicated. Mail to:

**HARLEQUIN
ROMANCE TREASURY
BOOK OFFER
P.O. BOX 1399
MEDFORD, N.Y. 11763, U.S.A.**

Make check or money order payable to: Harlequin Romance Treasury Offer. Allow 3 to 4 weeks for delivery.

Special offer expires: June 30, 1981.

PLEASE PRINT

Name

Address

Apt. No.

City

State/Prov.

Zip/Postal Code

Let Your Imagination Fly Sweepstakes

Rules and Regulations:

NO PURCHASE NECESSARY

1. Enter the Let Your Imagination Fly Sweepstakes 1, 2 or 3 as often as you wish. Mail each entry form separately bearing sufficient postage. Specify the sweepstake you wish to enter on the outside of the envelope. Mail a completed entry form or, your name, address, and telephone number printed on a plain 3"x 5" piece of paper to:
HARLEQUIN LET YOUR IMAGINATION FLY
SWEEPSTAKES,
P.O. BOX 1280, MEDFORD, N.Y. 11763 U.S.A.

2. Each completed entry form must be accompanied by I Let Your Imagination Fly proof-of-purchase seal from the back inside cover of specially marked Let Your Imagination Fly Harlequin books (or the words "Let Your Imagination Fly" printed on a plain 3"x 5" piece of paper. Specify by number the Sweepstakes you are entering on the outside of the envelope.

3. The prize structure for each sweepstake is as follows:

Sweepstake 1 – North America
Grand Prize winner's choice: a one-week trip for two to either Bermuda; Montreal, Canada; or San Francisco. 3 Grand Prizes will be awarded (min. approx. retail value $1,375. U.S., based on Chicago departure) and 4,000 First Prizes: scarves by nik nik, worth $14. U.S. each. All prizes will be awarded.

Sweepstake 2 – Caribbean
Grand Prize winner's choice: a one-week trip for two to either Nassau, Bahamas; San Juan, Puerto Rico; or St. Thomas, Virgin Islands. 3 Grand Prizes will be awarded. (Min. approx. retail value $1,650. U.S., based on Chicago departure) and 4,000 First Prizes: simulated diamond pendants by Kenneth Jay Lane, worth $15. U.S. each. All prizes will be awarded.

Sweepstake 3 – Europe
Grand Prize winner's choice: a one-week trip for two to either London, England; Frankfurt, Germany; Paris, France; or Rome, Italy. 3 Grand Prizes will be awarded. (Min. approx. retail value $2,800. U.S., based on Chicago departure) and 4,000 First Prizes: 1/2 oz. bottles of perfume, BLAZER by Anne Klein. (Retail value over $30. U.S.). All prizes will be awarded.

Grand trip prizes will include coach round-trip airfare for two persons from the nearest commercial airport serviced by Delta Air Lines to the city as designated in the prize, double occupancy accommodation at a first-class or medium hotel, depending on vacation, and $500. U.S. spending money. Departure taxes, visas, passports, ground transportation to and from airports will be the responsibility of the winners.

4. To be eligible, Sweepstakes entries must be received as follows:
Sweepstake 1 Entries received by February 28, 1981
Sweepstake 2 Entries received by April 30, 1981
Sweepstake 3 Entries received by June 30, 1981
Make sure you enter each Sweepstake separately since entries will not be carried forward from one Sweepstake to the next.

The odds of winning will be determined by the number of entries received in each of the three sweepstakes. Canadian residents, in order to win any prize, will be required to first correctly answer a time-limited skill-testing question, to be posed by telephone, at a mutually convenient time.

5. Random selections to determine Sweepstake 1, 2 or 3 winners will be conducted by Lee Krost Associates, an independent judging organization whose decisions are final. Only one prize per family, per sweepstake. Prizes are non-transferable and non-refundable and no substitutions will be allowed. Winners will be responsible for any applicable federal, state and local taxes. Trips must be taken during normal tour periods before June 30, 1982. Reservations will be on a space-available basis. Airline tickets are non-transferable, non-refundable and non-redeemable for cash.

6. The Let Your Imagination Fly Sweepstakes is open to all residents of the United States of America and Canada, (excluding the Province of Quebec) except employees and their immediate families of Harlequin Enterprises Ltd., its advertising agencies, Marketing & Promotion Group Canada Ltd. and Lee Krost Associates, Inc., the independent judging company. Winners may be required to furnish proof of eligibility. Void wherever prohibited or restricted by law. All federal, state, provincial and local laws apply.

7. For a list of trip winners, send a stamped, self-addressed envelope to:
Harlequin Trip Winners List, P.O. Box 1401, MEDFORD, N.Y. 11763 U.S.A.
Winners lists will be available after the last sweepstake has been conducted and winners determined.
NO PURCHASE NECESSARY.

Let Your Imagination Fly Sweepstakes

OFFICIAL ENTRY FORM

Please enter me in Sweepstake No. _____

Please print:
Name

Address

Apt. No.   City

State/   Zip/Postal
Prov.   Code

Telephone No.   area code
(   )

MAIL TO:
HARLEQUIN LET YOUR
IMAGINATION FLY SWEEPSTAKE No. _____
P.O. BOX 1280,
MEDFORD, N.Y. 11763 U.S.A.
(Please specify by number, the Sweepstakes you are entering.)